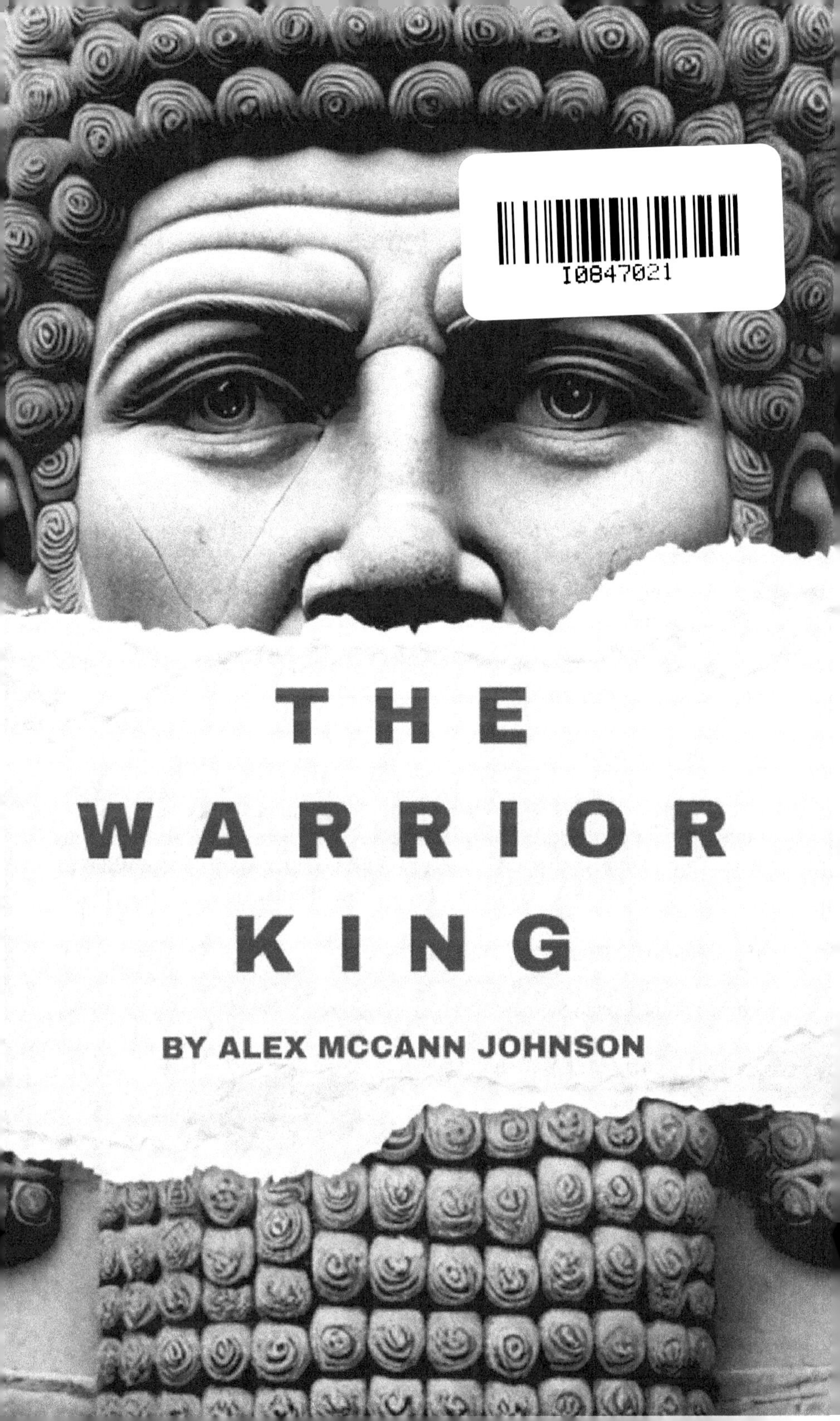

THE WARRIOR KING

BY ALEX MCCANN JOHNSON

The Warrior King

Alex McCann Johnson

Published by Guided by Spirit Publishing

Guided by Spirit Publishing
203 Main St.
Williston, ND, 58801, USA
www.guidedbyspiritpublishing.com
info@guidedbyspiritpublishing.com

Guided by Spirit Publishing
203 Main St.
Williston, ND, 58801, USA

The information in this book is provided for informational purposes only. The author and publisher make no representations as to the accuracy or completeness of any information in this book and are not liable for any errors or omissions or for the results obtained from the use of such information.

ISBN: 979-8-9913133-4-6

Printed in the United States of America

Cover Design by Alex McCann Johnson

Dedication

I have always had a love for writing the great myths. There is something powerful and eternal about the stories we inherit ,tales that breathe through time, teaching us about the lived experiences of those who came before us. Myths are more than echoes of the past. These stories are a lens through which we glimpse the magic of an era long gone and the truths that still live within us.

As I wrote this book, I held a quiet hope to give Gilgamesh and Enkidu the retelling they deserve. Their story, carved into ancient stone, continues to echo in the hearts of those who seek meaning, love, grief, and purpose. May this retelling honor their legend and keep their memory alive.

To one of the world's oldest written stories.

To Gilgamesh and Enkidu, this is for you.

To my loving husband, who always believes in me. He's my strength, my joy, and my home.

And to my amazing support system, thank you for lifting me when I needed wings.

Table of Contents

Prologue:

THE WILD MAN IS BORN

The gods convened in their celestial halls, their luminous forms etched against the vast expanse of the heavens. Their voices, both thunderous and melodic, echoed through the infinite void, each word a ripple across the fabric of creation. Mortal prayers had risen to their realm like an unrelenting tide, carried by the despair of the people of Uruk. Their cries spoke of suffering under the rule of Gilgamesh, the warrior king whose strength had grown unchecked, whose power had become a storm that battered his own people.

Anu, the king of the gods, sat upon his radiant throne, his expression as solemn as the laws that bound gods and men alike. "Gilgamesh," he began, his voice resonating like the toll of a great bell, "was born of divine intent, a child of Ninsun and Lugalbanda. Yet, his gifts have turned to excess. His strength has become a burden, his ambition a scourge. He oppresses the people he was destined to lead."

Ishtar, goddess of love and war, stepped forward, her beauty and fury entwined. Her eyes burned with a divine fire as her voice filled the assembly. "He builds walls that pierce the heavens and temples that gleam like the sun, yet he has forgotten why he rules. The people curse his name even as they admire his conquests. His heart is hardened, his spirit untamed. He must be tempered."

Ea, the god of wisdom, stroked his long beard, his gaze thoughtful. "To destroy him would undo the balance of the cosmos. He carries the blood of the gods, and his fate is bound to ours. Yet we cannot allow his tyranny to persist. We must forge a force to counter his might."

The gods murmured their agreement, their divine forms shimmering with the weight of the decision. Then, Aruru, the mother goddess and creator of humankind, stepped forward. Her voice carried the resonance of creation itself, each word infused with the power to shape the world.

"Let us create his equal," she declared. "A being born not of cities or temples but of the wilderness. Raw and untamed, he will challenge Gilgamesh's arrogance, test his strength, and teach him what it means to be mortal."

The assembly fell silent, the will of the gods now set. Aruru descended from the heavens, her form a beacon of divine purpose. She came to the wilderness, where the land remained untouched by mortal hands. The air was rich with the scent of ancient trees and wildflowers, and rivers roared with the vitality of life itself. It was here, by the banks of a mighty river, that Aruru knelt.

In her hands, she carried the sacred clay, damp with the waters of creation. With deft movements, she began to shape the form of a man. Her fingers molded broad shoulders, powerful limbs, and a face that was both fierce and noble. Her voice harmonized with the symphony of the wild. There was the rustling leaves, the flowing river, and the distant calls of birds.

"Rise from the earth," she whispered, her words a command that resonated through the elements. "Be as strong as the mountains, as swift as the rivers, as untamed as the wind. Let your spirit reflect the will of the gods, your heart remain bound to the earth."

The clay took shape under her touch, and when her work was complete, Aruru placed her hands over the figure's chest. She breathed the breath of life into him, and the clay transformed into flesh. The figure stirred, its chest rising with its first breath, and its eyes opened to the world.

Enkidu, the wild man, was born.

He rose to his full height, towering over the reeds and shrubs. His body was coiled with muscle, his form covered in hair as wild and dark as the shadows of the forest. Around him, the wilderness responded to his presence. Birds circled overhead, their cries jubilant. Deer and gazelles approached without fear, their trust in him instinctive and unshakable. Wolves gathered at a distance, their golden eyes reflecting his primal power.

Enkidu moved through the forest with wonder. He drank from rivers, marveling at his reflection in their mirrored surfaces. He ran alongside gazelles, his speed matching theirs, and hunted with wolves, his instincts sharp and precise. The wilderness was his home, his sanctuary, his kingdom.

Yet Enkidu was more than a beast. The spark of divinity within him gave him an awareness that transcended instinct. He observed the cycles of life and death, the delicate balance of creation and destruction. Though he could not yet articulate it, he sensed a greater purpose, a destiny beyond the forest.

His presence did not go unnoticed by mortal eyes. A hunter, skilled in reading the signs of the land, began to notice disruptions. Traps were sprung but left empty. The paths of animals had shifted, as if guided by an unseen force. One day, following a trail of broken reeds, the hunter came upon Enkidu.

The sight left him frozen with awe and terror. The wild man crouched by a river, his massive form illuminated by dappled sunlight. His movements were both graceful and powerful, his presence commanding. Around him, the animals gathered as though he were their king.

The hunter fled to Uruk, his heart racing as he recounted his tale to the priests. "I have seen a being born of the wild," he said, his voice trembling. "He runs with the beasts and commands them as though he were one of the gods."

The priests, wise in interpreting the will of the divine, understood the hunter's words. "This is no mere man," they said. "He is a creation of the gods, sent to balance Gilgamesh's strength. He must be brought to civilization."

The priests devised a plan and called upon Shamhat, a temple courtesan known for her wisdom, beauty, and grace. Her presence was said to soften even the hardest hearts, her voice a bridge between the realms of gods and men.

Guided by the hunter, Shamhat journeyed into the wilderness, carrying gifts of bread, wine, and honey. They found Enkidu by the river, crouched as he drank from its cool waters. When he sensed their presence, he turned, his piercing gaze meeting Shamhat's.

"You are mighty," Shamhat said, her voice steady and soothing. She extended her hands, offering the gifts she had brought. "But the gods have destined you for more. Come with me, and I will show you the world beyond these trees and rivers."

Enkidu hesitated, his instincts warring with the curiosity awakened by her words. Slowly, he approached, drawn by the promise of something beyond his understanding. In Shamhat's eyes, he saw not fear but recognition, a reflection of his own divinity.

Thus began Enkidu's journey from the wilds to the world of men, his path intertwined with that of Gilgamesh. Together, they would shape a story of strength and struggle, friendship and loss, a tale that would echo through the ages. For the gods had decreed it, and their will was written in the stars.

Chapter 1:

THE EPIC BEGINS

The city of Uruk sprawled beneath the relentless sun like a gleaming jewel of civilization, its grandeur a testament to human ambition and divine favor. From the towering heights of its walls thirty cubits high and wide enough to host races between chariots, one could survey the fertile plains cradled by the life-giving embrace of the Tigris and Euphrates rivers. These twin rivers, arteries of existence, carried more than water; they bore the stories of generations, whispers of gods and men alike. The walls themselves, smooth and radiant in the sunlight, were said to be the work of divine hands, their shimmering surfaces a beacon for travelers and a fortress against any who dared challenge Uruk's glory.

Within these walls lay the city's heartbeat, a labyrinth of bustling markets, sacred temples, and homes teeming with life. At its center stood the Eanna Temple, a monument to Ishtar, the goddess of love and war, its ziggurat rising like a celestial staircase. Each brick shimmered with the deep blue of lapis lazuli, seeming to touch the heavens themselves. Here, priests and priestesses performed sacred rites, their chants ascending with plumes of incense to the ears of the gods. Sacrifices were made with honeyed wine poured into carved basins, offerings of barley, lamb, and doves given to ensure the city's continued prosperity.

The streets below were alive with the pulse of trade and toil.

Merchants shouted their wares from stalls overflowing with silks dyed in vibrant indigos and crimsons, gold jewelry that caught the light like liquid fire, and spices that filled the air with the warmth of far-off lands. The clang of blacksmiths' hammers echoed as they forged bronze tools and weapons, while farmers guided carts laden with the fruits of their labor like dates, barley, and figs toward the central square. Uruk's people moved with purpose, their voices weaving into the symphony of a city that never rested.

Yet the crown of Uruk was not its walls or its temples, but its king. Gilgamesh, the man whose name carried the weight of legend. Born of Ninsun, a goddess of wisdom, and Lugalbanda, a mortal king, he was a figure of awe and contradiction, two-thirds divine, yet entirely human. His towering form cast a long shadow; his shoulders were broad enough to carry the weight of the city's hopes and fears, and his piercing eyes burned with a restless hunger. Clad in robes of purple and gold, he was both king and conqueror, a man whose deeds inspired songs yet whose actions sowed whispers of discontent.

In the grand halls of his palace, where carved pillars depicted the triumphs of gods and men, Gilgamesh sat upon a throne of ebony, its inlays of ivory and lapis glittering in the light of flickering torches. Around him, his advisors gathered, voices low with counsel and concern. They spoke of disputes over land, the need for new laws, and the murmurs of unrest among the people. Yet Gilgamesh listened with only half an ear. His fingers drummed the armrest, his gaze fixed on the horizon beyond the open windows, where the wilderness called to him with the allure of the unknown.

The king's restless energy had become both a boon and a curse. He had turned Uruk into a marvel of strength and beauty, but his ambition had no boundaries. He demanded more. He wanted the walls higher than the heavens, temples grander than those of his ancestors. He challenged the strongest of his subjects to contests of strength, defeating them with ease, leaving them broken and humiliated. He took from his people as if their lives were his to command, leaving fathers grieving, daughters shamed, and mothers weeping. The people bore their burdens in silence, but the discontent simmered beneath the surface.

The name Gilgamesh was known in Akkad, in Kish, in Lagash and beyond. When he marched with his armies, the earth itself seemed to tremble. He had conquered the hills and plains, seized temples and fortresses, and sent countless enemy warriors to their graves. His weapons, sharpened in battle, had cut through shields and flesh alike, and his voice had roared over the battlefield like thunder. His hands had built the walls of Uruk, but they had also torn lives apart without hesitation. He believed it was his right, as one favored above all men.

And yet, for all his strength, for all the feats that had inscribed his name into the songs of the land, he remained restless.

In the golden halls of his palace, where the flickering torchlight danced against walls inscribed with stories of his triumphs, his advisors and generals gathered to speak of the affairs of the city. They told of merchants petitioning for fairer taxes, of workers demanding rest from the king's relentless projects, of fathers who wished their daughters to be free of the shadow he cast upon them. But these words barely reached him. He listened, yet did not hear. His mind was always elsewhere, searching beyond the horizon, seeking a challenge that could truly test him.

He turned from his throne, his gaze drifting to the open archways of the palace, to the city beyond, to the plains that stretched far into the unknown. The walls he had built, meant to be his legacy, now seemed to confine him. The city he had made great no longer thrilled him. The people who called him king were nothing more than subjects to be ruled. His ambition had built Uruk, but it had also distanced him from the very lives he claimed dominion over.

"They grow weary of you, my king," one of his councilmen finally dared to say.

Gilgamesh turned slowly, his gaze falling upon the man. The silence that followed was heavy, suffocating. The councilman shifted under the weight of the king's stare, but he did not lower his head.

"Weary?" Gilgamesh echoed, his voice a slow, dangerous rumble.

"They fear you," the man continued, his voice carefully measured. "They whisper of your might, yes, but also of your will. They speak of your strength, but also of your burdens. The people of Uruk suffer under your hand."

A sharp breath filled the chamber. The other advisors tensed, their eyes darting between their king and the one who had spoken so boldly. No man had ever dared to voice such a thing to Gilgamesh before.

The king exhaled through his nose, stepping down from his throne, his heavy sandals striking the polished stone. "And what would they have me do?" he asked, his voice calm, but dangerous. "Would they have me lower these walls? Would they have me soften, let my enemies see weakness?"

"They would have you be a king," the councilman said. "Not a god."

A flicker of something passed over Gilgamesh's face, something unreadable, something almost human. But it was gone in an instant. He turned away from the council, stepping onto the balcony that overlooked his city.

Uruk sprawled before him, its streets pulsing with life, its buildings stretching toward the sky. He had made it great, carved it from the dust and shaped it into the heart of civilization. And yet, a strange feeling pressed against him, something he could not name.

Was he so above these people? Was he truly so far beyond them that he had become something else? It was like he was something more, but also something less?

No, he told himself. This city, this land, was his. The people were his. He had made them strong. They feared him because they should. He had no equal.

He would not falter. He would not bend.

And yet, the whisper of discontent had been planted, like a seed buried deep in the soil. One day, it would grow.

Chapter 2:

THE WARRIOR KING

The great hall of the palace shimmered with lavishness. Golden murals adorned the walls, each telling tales of conquests, of gods walking among mortals, and of a young king who had carved his name into the annals of history. The high, vaulted ceilings bore intricate carvings of celestial symbols, while massive bronze braziers cast flickering light over the gathered council. The air was thick with the scent of incense, and the low murmur of advisors mingled with the occasional clink of goblets filled with honeyed wine.

Gilgamesh reclined on his ebony throne. His dark, leonine hair fell in waves around his shoulders, and his piercing eyes surveyed the room with a mix of pride and boredom. Draped in robes of deep purple, embroidered with golden threads that caught the torchlight, he exuded an aura of power that was as undeniable as it was oppressive. His voice, when it came, was deep and commanding, carrying over the hushed conversations like a clarion call.

"Tell me," he began, leaning forward slightly, "why do the people of Uruk grumble like cattle in the fields? Why do they forget the battles I've fought, the victories I've won? Do they not remember that it is I who made this city great?"

His advisors, a mix of aging sages and sharp-eyed stewards, exchanged uneasy glances. None dared speak immediately, wary of their king's temper. At last, the man who had spoken the previous night named Kallum, who had served the court since Gilgamesh's father ruled, stepped forward. He bowed deeply, his silver hair catching the firelight.

"My king," Kallum began, his tone careful, "your victories are indeed the stuff of legend. No man, not even those blessed by the gods, could rival your strength or your valor in battle. But the people… they are as I've already said. Weary. They bear the weight of your ambitions."

Gilgamesh's eyes narrowed, his hand tightening around the armrest of his throne. "Weary?" he echoed, his voice sharp. "You already said this, yet I cannot see how? It was not them who has defeated enemies that would have surely killed them. It was not them who built the walls that they hide behind."

"They are proud of Uruk's splendor," Kallum replied, his voice steady despite the tension in the room. "But the labor to build it has left many broken. They toil endlessly, yet see little of the wealth their hands create."

Another advisor, younger and bolder, stepped forward. His name was Eshkar, a man known for his keen mind and willingness to speak plainly. "The men whisper of your contests of strength," he said. "They admire your prowess but resent the humiliation. They cannot match you, my king, and so they feel lesser. And the women…" Eshkar hesitated, choosing his words with care. "The women fear your gaze, for it is said that none may refuse the will of the king."

The hall fell silent, the weight of Eshkar's words hanging heavily in the air. Gilgamesh's jaw tightened, and for a moment, his advisors feared his wrath. Instead, he rose from his throne with a fluid grace, his towering form casting a long shadow across the room.

"Perhaps," he said, his voice quieter now, though no less commanding, "they have forgotten what it means to have a king like me. A king who is not only their ruler but their protector. Their warrior."

He began to pace, his strides long and purposeful. His advisors watched, unsure whether to speak or remain silent.

"Let me remind you all," Gilgamesh continued, his voice rising with each word, "of the battles I've fought and the blood I've spilled for this city. Do you remember the beasts of the southern marshes? The great lions that preyed upon our farmers, their roars shaking the earth? I faced them alone, armed only with my spear, and returned with their pelts to drape across these very walls."

He gestured toward one of the murals, which depicted a younger Gilgamesh standing triumphantly over the lifeless bodies of three massive lions. The artistry captured the ferocity of the beasts and the sheer power of the man who had slain them.

"And the mountain tribes," he continued, turning to face his council. "Those who dared to raid our caravans, stealing our grain and slaughtering our merchants. Did I not lead our armies into the mountains, where the air is thin and the paths treacherous? Did I not drive them from their caves and bring their leaders back in chains?"

The advisors murmured their agreement, nodding hesitantly. Gilgamesh's victories were undeniable, his feats unparalleled. But the tension in the room remained.

"My king," Kallum ventured cautiously, "your strength is indeed unmatched, and your deeds are worthy of song. Yet the people do not serve a king solely for his might. They seek fairness, wisdom, and compassion. They long for a ruler who sees their struggles, who understands their sacrifices."

Gilgamesh stopped pacing, his gaze locking onto the elder with an intensity that made the room feel colder despite the heat of the braziers. For a moment, it seemed as though he might lash out, but then his expression softened, barely.

"They are weak," he said, his tone dismissive. "They do not see that all I demand of them is for the glory of Uruk. They toil, yes, but they toil for a city that will stand for eternity, a city that even the gods will envy."

"Glory is a heavy burden, my king," Eshkar said quietly. "And even the strongest shoulders can falter beneath its weight."

Gilgamesh turned sharply toward the younger advisor, his eyes flashing. "Are you suggesting that I falter? That I, Gilgamesh, chosen of the gods, should lower myself to the level of those who serve me?"

"No, my king," Eshkar replied, his voice steady despite the dangerous edge in the air. "I suggest only that the people's faith in their king is their strength. And that faith, once lost, is hard to reclaim."

The hall fell silent again, the tension thick enough to cut. Gilgamesh's gaze swept over his council, taking in their bowed heads and wary expressions. For a moment, he seemed to wrestle with something unspoken, a flicker of doubt crossing his face before being replaced by his usual confidence.

"Enough," he said finally, his voice sharp. "Leave me. I will consider your words, though I doubt the people understand what it is to have a king such as I."

The advisors bowed deeply, retreating from the hall with murmured farewells. Once the massive doors closed behind them, Gilgamesh stood alone, the flickering torchlight casting shifting shadows across his face.

He turned to the mural of his triumphs, his gaze lingering on the depictions of battles fought and enemies vanquished. For the first time, the images did not fill him with pride but with a strange emptiness. He had built a legacy of strength and conquest, yet the whispers of his people gnawed at the edges of his thoughts.

"They forget," he muttered to himself, his voice low and tinged with frustration. "They forget what I have done for them."

Yet, as he stood there, a sliver of unease crept into his heart. Was it possible that strength alone was not enough? That his conquests, his monuments, his unyielding will, were these not the marks of a great king? Or had they become the very chains that bound his people in resentment?

15

Chapter 3:

THE DREAMS OF A KING

The night lay heavy, the heat wrapping itself around the city like a suffocating shroud. The bustling noise of the day had faded, leaving behind a quieter symphony with the occasional crackle of a torch, the murmurs of priests in the Eanna Temple, and the faint whispers of a breeze that stirred the thick air. Beneath the open expanse of a star-laden sky, the city's magnificence remained undiminished. The high walls, gilded by moonlight, stood as silent sentinels, and the grandeur of the palace loomed in the shadows. Yet within its opulent halls, a restless energy simmered.

Gilgamesh sat upright in his chamber, staring at the flickering light of a solitary lamp. The soft glow outlined the sharp planes of his face, his brow furrowed in thought. The weight of his dreams hung heavy over him, pressing down like an unseen force. For three nights, vivid and unrelenting visions had haunted his sleep, stirring emotions he had long buried. They were fear, awe, and an unsettling yearning he could neither name nor dismiss.

On the first night, the dream began in a barren expanse. The earth beneath him was cracked and lifeless, its dry surface stretching endlessly into the horizon. The air carried a suffocating stillness, and the sky above was a swirling mass of dark clouds, foreboding and impenetrable. In the distance, a mountain rose, jagged and immense, cloaked in mist that seemed alive, shifting and churning as though whispering secrets.

He walked forward, the ground trembling under his feet. Each step brought him closer to the mountain, and with it, a sense of both dread and inevitability. Then, from the mist, a figure emerged. Tall, powerful, and untamed, the man's presence was as commanding as a storm. His hair flowed like a lion's mane, wild and unyielding, and his eyes burned with an intensity that pierced Gilgamesh to his core. The figure raised a staff, its surface gnarled and alive, pulsating as if connected to the very earth itself.

"Who are you?" Gilgamesh demanded, his voice firm yet tinged with unease.

The figure said nothing, only stepped closer, his movements both deliberate and fluid. As he approached, the ground beneath Gilgamesh's feet split open with a deafening crack, and he plunged into a chasm of darkness.

The next morning, Gilgamesh had risen early, his jaw tight and his thoughts storming. He told no one of the dream, brushing off his advisors' concerns with curt dismissals. Yet, as night fell and the city of Uruk slumbered, the dream returned.

The second vision began atop the walls of Uruk. This time, the city was transformed. The vibrancy of its streets and the splendor of its temples were gone, replaced by an eerie silence. Shadows moved below, spectral forms drifting aimlessly. The figure from the first dream stood at the city's gates, his hand outstretched.

"Together, we will defy the gods," the figure said, his voice deep and resonant, echoing with an otherworldly power. "But first, you must learn the burden of mortality."

The words struck Gilgamesh like a blow. His pride bristled at the notion of defying the gods, yet something in the figure's gaze, steady and unyielding that planted a seed of curiosity within him.

The third night brought the most vivid dream yet. This time, Gilgamesh and the stranger stood side by side, their feet planted firmly in the earth. Before them loomed a monstrous beast, its eyes blazing like twin suns, its body massive and coiled with sinew. Flames licked from its jaws as it roared, shaking the very heavens. Without hesitation, Gilgamesh and the stranger charged, their voices raised in unison, their movements synchronized as if they had fought together a thousand times before.

When he awoke that morning, drenched in sweat, Gilgamesh could no longer deny the significance of these dreams. He summoned his mother, Ninsun, to the temple. Draped in shimmering robes that caught the light like the stars themselves, Ninsun entered with an air of calm divinity. She listened as her son recounted his visions, his voice steady yet tinged with urgency. Every detail fromevery crack in the earth, every word spoken by the figure, it was recounted with the precision of a man desperate for understanding.

When Gilgamesh finished, Ninsun regarded him with a gaze that seemed to pierce through the veil of mortal understanding. She stepped closer, placing a hand gently on his shoulder.

"The gods have spoken, my son," she said, her voice a balm against his restless spirit. "This figure you see is no ordinary man. He is crafted by the gods to be your equal in strength and spirit."

Gilgamesh's pride flared at her words, his fists clenching at the thought of an equal. Yet, deep within, a strange longing stirred, creating a yearning for something he could not yet name.

"And what of these dreams of defying the gods?" he asked, his voice sharp with challenge. "Do they mean to test me? Or to taunt me with a destiny I cannot escape?"

Ninsun's expression softened, and she reached out to cup his face. "The gods test all who are worthy of greatness," she said. "And you, my son, are destined for more than you can yet imagine. This wild man is both your challenge and your gift. Together, you will shape a story that will echo through the ages."

Gilgamesh said nothing, his jaw tight with the weight of her words. He turned away, his gaze falling to the altar of the temple. There, amidst the offerings of fruit, wine, and incense, he made a silent vow. Whatever the gods intended, he would meet it with the full force of his being.

As the day wore on, the city of Uruk thrummed with its usual energy, but within the palace, a storm brewed. Gilgamesh moved through the halls with a purpose that contradicted his inner turmoil. He gave orders to his advisors, commanded the priests to prepare the temples for further offerings, and paced the palace gardens, his thoughts consumed by the visions that had invaded his sleep.

For all his restlessness, there was a sense of anticipation building within him. He felt the pull of destiny, a thread woven by the gods, tugging him toward an unknown horizon. Somewhere beyond the walls of Uruk, the being from his dreams was waiting—a force of nature that would challenge everything he thought he knew about power, mortality, and the bonds that tether gods and men alike.

That night, as the stars began to emerge in the velvety expanse of the sky, Gilgamesh stood at the edge of his balcony, overlooking his city. The lights of Uruk flickered below, a reminder of the lives he ruled and the legacy he sought to build. The dreams had left him shaken, but they had also awakened something deeper, a fire that burned brighter than ever before.

For the first time in his life, Gilgamesh felt as though his story was no longer his alone. It was the beginning of something far greater, a chapter written not by his hand but by the will of the gods. And as the night deepened, the king of Uruk stood silent and still, his heart brimming with a restless anticipation that even he could not fully understand.

Chapter 4:

THE LINGERING ARRIVAL

Gilgamesh's sleep was restless, his dreams thick with imagery that pressed upon his mind like the heat of a summer storm. The flickering glow of the moonlight played on the walls of his chamber, its silvery sheen illuminating the contours of his restless form. As his body lay still, his mind was carried far from the confines of his palace, plunged into a vivid vision that spoke of gods and men, of wilderness and transformation.

He found himself standing on the edge of a vast forest, its canopy stretching endlessly, the trees thick with ancient wisdom. The air was alive with the scents of earth and rain, and the sounds of life pulsed in the distance, the birds calling to one another, the leaves rustling in the wind, and the deep, rhythmic growl of a river carving its way through the landscape. In this dream, Gilgamesh's feet felt the coolness of the soil, a sensation foreign to his existence in Uruk, where stone and heat reigned.

From the depths of the forest emerged a figure. Massive and primal, he moved with a grace that belied his sheer strength. His mane of hair shimmered like the pelt of a lion, his body clothed in nothing but the raw essence of the wild. Animals followed in his wake, the gazelles bounding alongside him, wolves trotting with deference, and birds wheeling overhead in joyous celebration. This was no ordinary man; he was something greater, something raw and untamed.

Gilgamesh spoke, his voice cutting through the dense air. "Who are you, creature of the forest? What is your purpose?"

The figure turned, his eyes meeting Gilgamesh's. In their depths was a power that rivaled the king's own. "I am of the earth," the figure replied, his voice deep as the rumble of thunder. "Born of clay and the breath of the gods. I am here because of you, Gilgamesh."

The words struck Gilgamesh like a blow, reverberating in the very core of his being. "Because of me? What do you mean?"

But the figure offered no further explanation. Instead, he moved closer, and with every step, the wild seemed to bleed into Gilgamesh's world. The trees grew taller, their roots spreading into the earth like veins. The animals drew closer, their eyes glowing with a strange, divine awareness.

Something was shifting.

The air grew still, and from the distance, another figure emerged. Her presence was deliberate, her beauty undeniable. She moved through the wilderness as though it belonged to her, as though she commanded the very heartbeat of nature itself. The trees did not whisper to her; they listened. The wind did not sweep past her, it lingered in her presence. She was neither predator nor prey, yet she held dominion over both.

Gilgamesh recognized her immediately. It was Shamhat, the priestess. She was clothed in fine linen, her arms adorned with golden bangles that caught the dappled light filtering through the canopy. In her hands, she carried gifts unlike any the wild man had ever seen. She had bread, warm and fragrant, and wine, dark and rich as the soil itself. She stepped forward without hesitation, closing the distance between them with measured grace.

"These are the gifts of civilization," she said, her voice soft but unwavering. "Eat, and you will begin to understand."

The wild man hesitated, his gaze flickering between her and the beasts who had gathered at the edge of the clearing. The wolves, the gazelles, the birds, they had been his kin, his companions, his only understanding of the world. The wilderness had claimed him, shaped him, made him strong. But now, something unfamiliar pressed against him, a force he could not name but could feel thrumming in his bones.

His fingers, rough from a life of survival, trembled as he reached forward. The warmth of the bread met his touch, foreign yet familiar, as though he had always known it, yet never dared to claim it. He tore a piece from the loaf and lifted it to his lips. As he chewed, the taste was unlike anything he had known. It was not the raw flesh of a fresh kill, not the bitter roots scavenged from the forest floor. It was something else entirely.

The change was instant, though subtle. He felt it in the way his shoulders, once hunched in readiness to pounce or flee, began to relax. His breath, always shallow and quick, slowed. The gnawing hunger that had driven every action of his life dulled, not just in his stomach but in his very being. The world shifted around him, the edges of his existence fraying, reshaping.

The beasts sensed it before he did.

The wolves, once his brothers in the hunt, slunk back into the shadows of the trees, their golden eyes lingering on him for a moment before they disappeared. The gazelles, who had once grazed fearlessly at his side, bounded away, their slender legs carrying them deeper into the safety of the wilderness. The birds, which had filled the air with their endless chatter, suddenly took flight, their wings cutting through the sky as if severing a bond that had once tied them together.

The air itself seemed to recoil, as though the land recognized that he no longer belonged to it.

He straightened, his movements slower, more deliberate. His stance shifted, losing the primal crouch that had defined him for so long. He looked down at his hands. They were scarred, calloused, covered in the dirt of the untamed world. He and saw them differently for the first time. They were not claws. They were hands. Hands that could build, that could shape, that could grasp more than just the next meal.

Shamhat watched him, her expression unreadable but patient. "Drink," she said, offering him the wine.

He took the cup, his fingers tightening around the smooth surface. The scent was rich, intoxicating in a way he had never known. He lifted it to his lips, the liquid washing over his tongue, filling his chest with warmth that spread outward, seeping into every limb. It was not merely drink, it was a baptism, a cleansing of the past.

He exhaled slowly.

Something had changed.

He could not name it, could not yet understand it, but he felt it. The wildness had not left him, not entirely. It still simmered beneath the surface, a whisper rather than a roar. But he was no longer only that. He had stepped across the threshold between the world he had known and the one that awaited him.

Shamhat smiled, not in victory, but in recognition. She had not broken him; she had merely guided him to a door he had never known existed. It was he who had chosen to step through it.

"There is more," she said gently. "More than the hunt. More than the night and the chase. More than hunger and survival. You will see."

The wild man, who was now something more, something in between, nodded. He did not know what awaited him beyond this place, beyond this moment, but he knew that there was no turning back.

The forest, which had once been his home, now looked

different.

Smaller.

He took a deep breath and stepped forward.

The dream shifted abruptly. Gilgamesh now stood on the walls of Uruk, looking down at his city. He had just realized that he had felt almost as if he were in Enkidu's perspective before, yet now he had returned to his body. In the distance, he saw the figure of the wild man approaching, Shamhat at his side. Behind them lay the wilderness, fading into the horizon as though consumed by the encroachment of man. The sight filled Gilgamesh with both anticipation and unease. He felt an invisible tether binding him to the approaching figure, a connection that defied logic but resonated deeply within his chest.

"You will meet him," a voice echoed, reverberating through the dreamscape. It was the voice of Ninsun, his mother, her tone steady and sure. "He is your equal, sent to balance your strength and guide your ambition. He will be your companion, your rival, and your greatest ally."

The words lingered in his mind as the vision dissolved, the forest and the walls of Uruk fading into darkness. Gilgamesh awoke with a sharp intake of breath, his heart pounding as though he had run for miles. The chamber was quiet save for the faint hum of the night breeze slipping through the open windows. He sat up, the dream vivid in his mind, each detail etched with the clarity of prophecy.

He rose from his bed, draping a robe of deep indigo over his shoulders, and strode to the temple where Ninsun resided. The moonlight guided his steps, its glow illuminating the intricate carvings of the temple walls. Inside, the air was cool and heavy with the scent of incense, the flickering light of oil lamps casting shifting shadows.

Ninsun stood before an altar, her presence serene yet

commanding. She turned as her son approached, her eyes reflecting both love and the wisdom of the divine. "You have dreamed again," she said, her tone making it a statement rather than a question.

Gilgamesh nodded, his expression troubled. "I saw him, Mother. The wild man. He is no ordinary creature. He is something greater, something born of the gods."

Ninsun gestured for him to sit beside her, her movements deliberate and calm. "He is Enkidu," she said. "The gods have created him as your equal. He will challenge you, temper you, and reveal truths you have yet to face. His arrival is the will of the heavens."

Gilgamesh's pride bristled, his jaw tightening. "An equal? What equal could there be to me, the son of a goddess, the strongest of men?"

Ninsun placed a hand on his shoulder, her touch gentle yet firm. "Strength is not merely the power of the body, my son. It is the capacity to grow, to learn, and to understand. Enkidu's strength is different from yours, but no less formidable. Through him, you will come to know yourself."

The words settled over Gilgamesh like a weight, both comforting and burdensome. He looked into his mother's eyes, searching for answers to the questions that churned within him. "What is my path, then? What am I to do when I meet him?"

"You will know," Ninsun said simply, her gaze unwavering. "The gods have set this course for both of you. Trust in their will, and in your own heart."

Chapter 5:

A CLASH OF WILLS

The great city hummed under the midmorning sun, a cacophony of life teeming within its high walls. Merchants called out from their stalls, hawking everything from jars of fragrant oils to finely woven silks dyed in vibrant hues. Priests tended to altars, their chants rising in a melodic rhythm, mixing with the clatter of pottery and the calls of laborers hauling goods to the bustling market square. Children wove through the crowds with playful energy, their laughter a bright counterpoint to the murmurs of whispers spreading like wildfire through the streets.

The whispers carried the tale of a wild man, a being forged by the gods, born of the wilderness, and imbued with a strength that rivaled the mighty Gilgamesh. They said he had been sent to challenge the king, to temper his unchecked ambition, and restore balance to the lives of Uruk's people. Some saw it as a warning, others as salvation. The uncertainty hung in the air, sharpening the anticipation that gripped the city.

At the palace gates, Gilgamesh leaned against a carved pillar, his eyes scanning the horizon. The sharp lines of his jaw tightened as he considered the rumors. A wild man? Sent to challenge him? He smirked, his pride swelling. The gods had often tested him, and he had triumphed each time. He was Gilgamesh, king of Uruk, child of divinity, the builder of walls that pierced the heavens. No man, mortal or otherwise, could match him.

And yet, a flicker of unease lingered in the back of his mind. He had dreamed of this moment, seen glimpses of a figure who moved with the force of a storm. The dream had left him restless, its images vivid and persistent. He had spoken of it to his mother, Ninsun, who had confirmed his suspicions with a calm certainty. "This wild man, this Enkidu, will change you. He is your equal, your shadow, your reflection."

The crowd's murmurs grew louder, pulling Gilgamesh's attention to the commotion stirring at the edge of the market. The throng parted like water before a great wave, and then he saw him. Enkidu.

He moved through the streets with a commanding presence, his massive frame draped in raw power. His wild mane of hair caught the sunlight, gleaming like spun gold, and his piercing eyes scanned his surroundings with a mix of curiosity and determination. The wilderness seemed to linger in his steps, the wild essence clinging to him like a second skin. Behind him, Shamhat walked with quiet grace, her steady presence tempering the primal energy radiating from him.

Gilgamesh straightened, his muscles coiling with anticipation. Here was a man who did not cower, whose steps carried purpose and defiance. For the first time in years, the king felt a spark of something unfamiliar. It was a mix of excitement, tempered by a curiosity that burned like embers in his chest.

Enkidu stopped at the foot of the palace steps, his gaze locking with Gilgamesh's. The air between them crackled with unspoken energy, their destinies colliding in a moment that silenced even the wind.

"Are you the one they call Gilgamesh?" Enkidu's voice was deep and steady, carrying across the square with ease.

Gilgamesh descended the steps, his movements deliberate,

his piercing gaze never leaving Enkidu. "I am," he replied, his voice filled with pride. "King of Uruk. Builder of its walls. Chosen of the gods."

"And I am Enkidu," the wild man said, his tone unyielding. "Born of the earth, forged by the gods. I have come to meet you, king. To see if the strength of a man can match the power of the wild."

The words hung in the air like a challenge, and the crowd tensed, holding its collective breath. Gilgamesh's lips curved into a faint smile, though his eyes glinted with a sharp edge. "You think yourself my equal, Enkidu? Prove it."

Enkidu's stance shifted, a faint smile mirroring Gilgamesh's own. "It is not I who needs proving."

The crowd fell silent as Gilgamesh and Enkidu faced one another, the tension between them thick as the heat of the noonday sun. Around them, the people of Uruk watched with wide eyes, their breath held in anticipation of what was to come. The king of Uruk and the wild man, equal in stature and power, had locked eyes, their destinies entwined in a way that none present could fully comprehend.

Without warning, Gilgamesh moved. His body, honed by years of battle, was a blur of motion as he lunged at Enkidu, his fists clenched and his muscles rippling with divine strength. Enkidu met him head-on, his instincts born of the wilderness guiding him. Their collision sent a thunderous boom through the square, the impact shaking the very stones beneath their feet.

The fight was a clash of two worlds, civilization and the wild. Gilgamesh's strikes were precise, calculated, and devastating. Each blow was delivered with the force of a seasoned warrior, his movements like a symphony of violence. Enkidu countered with raw power and primal ferocity, his every move a reflection of the untamed wilderness that had shaped him. Where Gilgamesh was methodical, Enkidu was unpredictable, his attacks flowing like water, surging like a river over stone.

Gilgamesh feinted left, his eyes narrowing as he sought an opening. Enkidu anticipated the move, pivoting with a speed that belied his massive frame. The wild man's hand shot out, catching Gilgamesh's arm mid-strike, and with a roar, he twisted, throwing the king into the dirt. The crowd gasped as Gilgamesh rolled to his feet, undeterred, his lips curling into a grin.

"You're strong," Gilgamesh said, his voice carrying over the stunned silence of the square. "But strength alone will not bring you victory."

Enkidu's expression remained calm, though his eyes burned with a fierce determination. "Strength is not all I carry, Gilgamesh," he replied. "The earth moves in me, as do the winds and the rivers. Show me if you can match them."

The two circled one another, their movements slow and deliberate, the air between them charged with anticipation. Then, as if driven by the same unspoken signal, they surged forward again. Fists met flesh, the crack of their strikes echoing through the air. Enkidu's raw power sent Gilgamesh staggering back, but the king recovered quickly, using his agility to dodge a second strike before countering with a crushing blow to Enkidu's ribs.

The wild man grunted but did not falter. Instead, he charged, his shoulder connecting with Gilgamesh's chest and driving the king back several steps. The force was immense, but Gilgamesh dug his heels into the ground, halting Enkidu's momentum. With a growl, he hooked his arm around Enkidu's neck, twisting his body and pulling the wild man down into a grapple. The two titans crashed to the ground, their bodies tangled as they struggled for dominance.

Dust rose around them in thick clouds as they wrestled, each refusing to yield. Gilgamesh's hands found Enkidu's shoulders, his grip ironclad as he forced the wild man down. But Enkidu, with the raw strength of the wilderness coursing through him, pushed back, his muscles straining as he began to rise.

"You're relentless," Gilgamesh said through gritted teeth, his face inches from Enkidu's. "I've never faced anyone like you."

"Perhaps it is because you've never faced your equal," Enkidu replied, his voice steady despite the strain of their battle.

With a sudden burst of power, Enkidu flipped Gilgamesh onto his back, pinning him for a heartbeat before the king twisted free. They scrambled to their feet, their chests heaving as they stared at each other. Sweat slicked their skin, their muscles gleamed in the sunlight, and the crowd remained enraptured, their cheers forgotten in the awe of the spectacle.

Gilgamesh attacked again, this time with a flurry of strikes that drove Enkidu back toward the edge of the square. The wild man blocked and dodged where he could, his movements quick and fluid. But Gilgamesh's strikes were relentless, each one designed to wear down his opponent. Finally, Enkidu saw his opening. As Gilgamesh raised his arm for another strike, Enkidu stepped in, catching the king's wrist and twisting. With a roar, he threw Gilgamesh over his shoulder, sending him crashing to the ground.

For a moment, it seemed as though the wild man had won. But Gilgamesh, undeterred, surged to his feet once more. His grin returned, wider this time, and his eyes sparkled with something unexpected, respect.

"You fight with the spirit of a lion," Gilgamesh said, his voice filled with admiration. "I have faced armies, beasts, and the wrath of the gods, but never have I faced anyone like you."

Enkidu inclined his head, his breathing heavy but steady. "And you are more than the stories I've heard, Gilgamesh. Your strength is not merely of the body but of the spirit. You fight with purpose."

The two men lunged at each other again, their bodies colliding in a final, monumental clash. The ground beneath them seemed to tremble with the force of their struggle. Gilgamesh used his agility to maneuver behind Enkidu, locking his arms around the wild man's torso and lifting him from the ground. With a mighty roar, Gilgamesh slammed Enkidu to the earth, pinning him with all his strength.

Enkidu struggled, his muscles coiling like snakes beneath Gilgamesh's grip. But this time, the king held firm, his hands pressing Enkidu's shoulders into the dirt. They locked eyes, their breaths labored, their bodies exhausted.

"I yield," Enkidu said finally, his voice calm and unwavering.

Gilgamesh released him, stepping back and extending a hand to help him rise. The crowd erupted into cheers, their voices filling the square like a tide. The two men stood side by side, their expressions softened by the understanding that had passed between them.

"You are not my enemy," Gilgamesh said, his voice carrying over the crowd. "You are my equal, my brother. The gods have sent you to me not as a rival, but as a companion. You fought well, friend."

"And you, Gilgamesh," Enkidu replied, his hand gripping the king's firmly, "are the one I was destined to meet."

Chapter 6:
THE BOND BETWEEN MAN AND BEAST

The city of Uruk had never known a moment like this. The meeting of Gilgamesh and Enkidu, a clash of unparalleled strength and will, had left an unforgettable mark on its people. The ground had quaked beneath their struggle, but it was the bond that followed, unexpected and profound, that truly captured their imagination. In the days after their legendary encounter, the wild man and the king became inseparable. Where once the citizens of Uruk whispered of Gilgamesh's tyranny, they now spoke in awe of the partnership that had emerged, a connection blessed, or perhaps ordained, by the gods themselves.

Their bond deepened swiftly. To Gilgamesh, Enkidu was not merely a rival or companion; he was a reflection of his own power, someone who forced him to confront the edges of his strength and the weight of his pride. For Enkidu, Gilgamesh was a guide to the complexities of human ambition and civilization, a living embodiment of both divine gifts and mortal flaws. Together, they began to explore not only the depths of their strength but the possibilities of their shared existence.

Uruk thrived under their dual presence. In the mornings, the city buzzed with the sound of their sparring in the palace courtyard. Their battles drew crowds, the citizens of Uruk watching with breathless awe as the two titans faced off, their strikes so powerful they seemed to shake the air. Gilgamesh, accustomed to victory, found himself tested in ways he had never known, while Enkidu's wild strength grew sharper and more disciplined under Gilgamesh's guidance. Each clash ended with laughter and clasped hands, a testament to the trust that had begun to bloom between them.

When they weren't training, they roamed the city together. Gilgamesh delighted in showing Enkidu the wonders of Uruk, from the towering ziggurat of Ishtar gleaming under the sun, to the bustling markets where merchants bartered for spices and silks, and even the mighty walls that stood as a testament to his ambition. Enkidu, wide-eyed and curious, absorbed it all. His questions were endless, and Gilgamesh answered them with a pride that bordered on joy.

Yet it wasn't just the grandeur of the city that captivated Enkidu. It was the people. In the evenings, he and Gilgamesh sat with farmers and artisans, listening to their stories, laughing at their jokes. For Enkidu, who had known only the solitude of the wilderness, the warmth of community was a revelation. Even Gilgamesh, who had ruled over these people for years, began to see them through Enkidu's eyes. The weight of his kingship shifted, lightened by a newfound connection to the lives he had so often overlooked.

But their newfound bond was soon tested. Trouble had come to the outskirts of Uruk, spreading fear like wildfire. Farmers spoke of a lion larger than any they had ever seen, its golden mane darkened by a shadow that seemed to move with unnatural intent. The beast had begun attacking livestock, then people. The villagers whispered that it was no ordinary animal, but a creature of divine wrath, sent to punish them for their sins.

When word reached the palace, Gilgamesh and Enkidu wasted no time. They armed themselves and set out, leaving the walls of Uruk behind to confront the beast. The journey across the plains was uneventful, the sun high and the air heavy with heat. But as they neared the area where the lion had last been seen, an unnatural stillness fell over the land. The usual sounds of the plains like chirping insects and the rustling grass, were gone, replaced by a silence so thick it felt alive.

Gilgamesh paused, his hand resting on the hilt of his sword. "Do you feel it?" he asked, his voice low.

Enkidu nodded, his keen senses on edge. "The air is wrong. This is no ordinary lion."

They followed the trail of destruction. It started with a path of crushed grass and shattered trees and went to the remnants of a shepherd's flock strewn like broken toys. The ground itself bore the marks of the beast's passage, deep gouges where its claws had torn through the earth. As they advanced, the silence was broken by a low growl, a sound that seemed to rise from the depths of the earth itself.

The lion emerged from the shadows, its size dwarfing even the largest of its kind. Its golden coat shimmered unnaturally, and its eyes glowed with a malevolent light. But it was the shadow beneath it that struck fear into even Gilgamesh's heart. It moved independently, shifting and twisting as if alive, its edges blurred and shifting like smoke.

Gilgamesh drew his sword, its blade catching the sunlight. "Whatever you are," he called, his voice steady, "you will not harm my people again."

The lion roared, the sound reverberating across the plains. It charged, its massive form moving with terrifying speed. Gilgamesh met it head-on, his sword slicing through the air. The blade struck true, but the shadow twisted around it, dulling the blow. Enkidu leapt into the fray, his raw strength meeting the beast's fury. He wrestled with the lion, his arms straining as he held its snapping jaws at bay.

The battle raged, a primal clash that shook the earth. The lion's strength was unnatural, its movements impossibly fast and precise. It struck with claws like daggers, tearing through the air with a force that sent shockwaves through the ground. Gilgamesh and Enkidu fought as one, their movements perfectly synchronized. Where Gilgamesh struck with precision, Enkidu countered with raw power, their partnership a seamless dance of strength and skill.

Despite their unity, the lion's shadow proved a formidable foe. It moved with a will of its own, striking out like a living thing. It coiled around Gilgamesh's legs, pulling him to the ground, and lashed at Enkidu, its tendrils leaving jagged wounds that burned like fire.

Gilgamesh gritted his teeth, his body thrumming with divine energy. He rose to his feet, his sword flashing as he drove the shadow back. "It's more than flesh and blood!" he called to Enkidu. "We must strike together!"

Enkidu nodded, his eyes blazing with determination. He gripped the lion's mane, forcing its head upward, exposing its throat. "Now, Gilgamesh!"

With a roar, Gilgamesh charged, his sword glowing with the light of the sun. He plunged the blade deep into the lion's neck, the force of the strike sending a shockwave through the beast. The lion roared in agony, its shadow twisting and writhing before finally dissolving into the air. The beast collapsed, its massive body falling still.

The plains fell silent once more.

Gilgamesh and Enkidu stood over the fallen lion, their chests heaving. Blood stained their arms, their faces marked with exhaustion, but their eyes were alight with victory. Gilgamesh placed a hand on Enkidu's shoulder, a grin breaking across his face.

"Together, we are unstoppable," he said. "Imagine if the gods themselves chose to face us. They would piss themselves at the sight of us."

Enkidu returned the smile, his grip firm as they clasped hands. "I fear you will anger them soon enough. This was no ordinary beast. The gods must be testing us."

Gilgamesh nodded, his gaze turning to the horizon. "If this was a test, then we have passed it. But I suspect our trials are only beginning."

When they returned to Uruk, the lion's massive pelt draped across their shoulders, the city erupted in celebration. The people cheered their king and his companion, their fears replaced by awe. No longer did they speak of weariness. Gilgamesh and Enkidu stood as symbols of hope.

That night, as the fires of celebration burned bright, Gilgamesh and Enkidu sat together, the lion's pelt spread beneath them. The feast had begun to wind down, though laughter and song still echoed across the city. Servants moved between the guests, refilling goblets of wine, while musicians plucked melodies that danced in the night air. The scent of roasted meat lingered, mingling with the faint perfume of myrrh that smoldered in the bronze censers.

But amidst all the revelry, Gilgamesh felt as though the world had shrunk to just this moment. It was just the warmth of the fire, the taste of wine on his tongue, and the presence of the man beside him that brought him to a state of presence.

He turned his gaze toward Enkidu, who sat relaxed, his wild curls tousled from the night's revels, his strong frame draped in a loose tunic that did little to conceal the power beneath. His laughter was uninhibited, unburdened by the weight of kingship or conquest. The flickering fire cast golden light across his skin, highlighting the rugged beauty that had not diminished despite his time away from the wild.

Gilgamesh had seen Enkidu in battle, had watched him fight with the strength of a storm, his movements fierce and untamed. He had seen him challenge gods and men alike, standing firm with unshaken resolve. And yet, here, in the quiet hum of the night, he saw another side of him, something softer, something raw.

He did not know what it was that stirred within him, only

that it was different from anything he had felt before.

Gilgamesh had known admiration. He had known loyalty, had known the unbreakable bond forged between warriors who had stood shoulder to shoulder against death. But this was something else. It was not just the thrill of victory or the comfort of companionship. It was something deeper, something unspoken.

Enkidu turned to him then, his smile lazy with contentment, the warmth of the wine bringing a flush to his cheeks. "You are quiet, my king," he said, tilting his head in amusement. "Does Uruk's great lion not revel in his own triumphs?"

Gilgamesh smirked, lifting his goblet in a mock toast. "Perhaps the lion is tired," he mused. "Or perhaps he finds more pleasure in the company he keeps than in the victory itself."

Enkidu chuckled, taking a slow sip of his wine. "Then tonight, the lion rests. He has earned it."

Gilgamesh held his gaze for a moment longer than he intended. The firelight danced in Enkidu's eyes, reflecting something that made Gilgamesh's heart hammer a little harder against his ribs. He wanted to say something, to name the feeling that curled in his chest, to put into words the warmth that spread through him whenever Enkidu was near.

But he did not.

He looked away, tilting his goblet to his lips and drinking deeply. The wine was sweet, but it did not drown the ache of the unspoken.

Chapter 7:

THE CEDAR FOREST

The idea of the Cedar Forest quest took root on a restless night in Uruk, with Gilgamesh and Enkidu seated beneath the vast expanse of stars on the palace terrace. The night air was warm, laced with the faint scent of jasmine that drifted up from the royal gardens below. The city, usually alive with sound, lay quieter than usual. Only the occasional bark of a distant dog or the muffled hum of late-night revelers disturbed the serene silence. Above them, the heavens stretched endlessly, the stars flickering like embers against the black velvet of the sky.

Gilgamesh leaned back on his hands, his gaze fixed on the constellations above. His restlessness was palpable, a tension that hummed beneath his skin. It was a familiar feeling, one that had driven him to build Uruk's mighty walls, to wrestle with Enkidu, and to claim victories that no other man could dream of. But tonight, even the grandeur of his accomplishments felt hollow.

"The gods have given me strength," Gilgamesh began, his voice breaking the silence. It was low but carried a weight that immediately drew Enkidu's attention. "They have made me the greatest of men. Yet for what purpose? To build walls, to conquer rivals? These things are fleeting, like the wind that carries the desert sands. What is the worth of my power if it is never tested against the impossible?"

Enkidu, seated beside him, tilted his head in thought. His wild mane of hair caught the faint light of the moon, his sharp features shadowed but calm. "You have already bested the strongest men," he replied evenly. "Even I, born of the wilderness, could not defeat you. I am your greatest feat. What challenge could surpass what you have already achieved?"

Gilgamesh turned to his companion, his eyes gleaming with the fire of ambition. "The Cedar Forest," he said, his voice rising with excitement. "It is no ordinary place. It is a land of legend, guarded by Humbaba, the terror of the gods. They say no man who enters the forest returns. But we are not ordinary men, Enkidu. If we defeat Humbaba, our names will echo through eternity."

Enkidu's expression darkened. The Cedar Forest was no myth to him; its shadow had loomed over the wild lands he once called home. He had heard the whispers of hunters who spoke of it with dread, their voices trembling as they described the horrors said to lurk within. "Humbaba is no mere foe," he said quietly, his tone laced with caution. "He is the wrath of the gods incarnate, placed there by Enlil himself to guard the sacred forest. To face him is to risk the fury of the divine."

Gilgamesh's grin widened, undeterred by his companion's warning. "All the more reason to go," he countered, his voice brimming with resolve. "The gods gave us strength and free will. If we do not use these gifts to carve our own destiny, we are no better than the beasts of the field."

Enkidu studied him for a long moment, his heart caught between the caution of his instincts and the loyalty that bound him to the king. Gilgamesh's fire was infectious, his determination a force that seemed to pull at the threads of fate itself. At last, Enkidu nodded. "If this is the path you have chosen," he said, his voice steady, "then I will walk it with you. But understand this and be wary. Humbaba is more than a guardian. He is the forest, its fury and its spirit."

"Then together, we will face him," Gilgamesh declared,

clapping a hand on Enkidu's shoulder. "We will return with Humbaba's head, and the world will remember our names forever."

The very next day, Gilgamesh's court buzzed with anticipation as preparations for the journey began. Weapons were sharpened, provisions packed, and prayers offered at the temple of Ishtar. The people gathered in the streets to watch as their king and his companion prepared to leave. Gilgamesh stood clad in gleaming armor that caught the light of the rising sun. Beside him, Enkidu stood unadorned, his strength and calm presence speaking volumes without need for embellishment.

As the gates of Uruk closed behind them, the two men set out, their path stretching into the horizon. The journey was long and arduous, taking them across rolling plains, jagged hills, and eventually into the shadow of towering mountains. Each night, they camped beneath the stars, their conversations weaving tales of ambition, dreams, and memories. Gilgamesh spoke often of immortality, of a legacy so vast that even the gods would take notice. Enkidu, in turn, shared his reverence for life itself, painting vivid pictures of its beauty and its perils.

As they drew closer to the Cedar Forest, the air began to change. It grew thick with the heady scent of cedar, a fragrance both alluring and ominous. The trees rose like giants on the horizon, their massive trunks cloaked in shadow. Even from a distance, the forest seemed alive, its edges shifting as though it breathed with an ancient, unseen power.

Enkidu slowed as they approached, his gaze scanning the dense canopy that loomed ahead. "This is a cursed place," he said softly, his voice carrying an edge of unease. "The forest watches us. Humbaba's presence is everywhere."

Gilgamesh tightened his grip on his sword, his jaw set in determination. "Let him watch," he said. "We did not come this far to turn back now."

As they crossed the threshold into the Cedar Forest, the

atmosphere grew oppressive. The shadows seemed to stretch and shift, their movements deliberate and unnerving. The usual sounds of a forest were absent, replaced by an eerie silence that pressed against their senses. Each step felt heavier, the weight of divine judgment hanging in the air.

"This place is alive," Enkidu murmured, his voice barely audible. "It is not just trees and soil. It is the will of the gods, and it does not welcome us."

Gilgamesh pressed forward, his resolve unshaken. "Then let it challenge us," he replied. "We will meet its fury head-on."

The deeper they ventured, the more the forest seemed to close in around them. The massive cedar trees towered above, their branches intertwining to form a dense, impenetrable canopy. Light filtered through in faint, golden streaks, casting the forest floor in shifting patterns. The scent of cedar was overpowering now, thick and intoxicating, filling their lungs with every breath.

Then, in the stillness, a sound emerged. It was a low, rumbling rumble that seemed to vibrate through the very ground beneath their feet. It grew louder, a guttural roar that shook the air and sent a flock of unseen birds scattering into the canopy. Enkidu froze, his muscles tensing. "He knows we are here," he said grimly.

Gilgamesh raised his sword, his eyes scanning the dense undergrowth. "Good," he said, his voice steady. "Let him come."

The forest fell silent once more, the calm before the storm.

Chapter 8

THE SPIRIT OF THE FOREST

The air in the Cedar Forest was electric, thrumming with an ancient power that seemed to emanate from the very roots of the towering trees. Every creak of the branches, every whisper of the wind, felt deliberate, as though the forest itself watched Gilgamesh and Enkidu with a sentient malice. The thick scent of cedar clung to the air, sharp and oppressive, mingling with the tension that tightened around them like a vice. The two companions stood ready, their weapons gleaming faintly in the filtered light that struggled through the dense canopy.

Then Humbaba appeared.

He emerged from the shadows like a living nightmare, his colossal form nearly as tall as the tallest trees. His skin, textured and gnarled like ancient bark, seemed to shift and writhe as though it were part of the forest itself. His eyes burned with an unnatural light, twin orbs of molten fury that seared through the dimness. His breath came in great, heaving gusts that stirred the forest around him, each exhale carrying the scent of decay and life entwined.

Gilgamesh's grip on his sword tightened, the bronze blade catching what little light filtered through the dense canopy. Enkidu stood beside him, his club poised, his muscles taut as a bowstring. The two men exchanged a glance, an unspoken understanding passing between them. This was no ordinary battle. This was a clash with a force of nature.

"You dare intrude upon my forest?" Humbaba's voice rolled through the woods, deep and resonant, like a storm reverberating across the earth. "You trespassers, you insects! Did you think the gods would spare you for this arrogance?"

"We came knowing the risks," Gilgamesh replied, his voice steady, though his heart pounded. "We are here to face you, Humbaba, and to claim the Cedar Forest for ourselves."

Humbaba laughed, a sound like thunder splitting the sky. "Fools! I am the forest. My roots reach deep into the earth; my limbs stretch to the heavens. You fight not just me but the will of Enlil himself."

With that, Humbaba raised one massive arm, and the forest responded. The ground beneath Gilgamesh and Enkidu trembled, roots surging from the soil like living serpents. They lashed out, coiling and snapping toward the intruders. Enkidu reacted first, his instincts honed by years in the wild. He dodged a thick root that shot toward his legs, swinging his club to sever it with a satisfying crack. The root writhed and recoiled, the ground beneath it bleeding dark sap.

Gilgamesh was less agile but no less determined. A root coiled around his ankle, its grip tightening with crushing force. With a roar, he drove his sword into it, the blade slicing through the gnarled wood. The root released him with a shudder, retreating into the ground. But the attack was far from over.

Humbaba moved with startling speed for his size, his massive limbs tearing through the forest as if it bent to his will. He swung one arm in a wide arc, and the air itself seemed to split. The force of the blow sent both men sprawling, the ground beneath them cracking with the impact. Above them, the trees swayed violently, their branches creaking and groaning as though in protest.

"Enkidu!" Gilgamesh shouted, his voice strained as he

scrambled to his feet. "The forest fights with him."

Enkidu nodded, his breath heavy but his resolve unshaken. "The trees are his soldiers," he said, his voice grim. "We must outthink him, not just overpower him."

Humbaba let out another guttural roar, his molten eyes narrowing as he raised both arms. The trees responded, their massive branches swaying and creaking as they descended toward Gilgamesh and Enkidu like crushing hammers. Enkidu darted to the side, his movements fluid and precise, while Gilgamesh rolled beneath one of the massive limbs, narrowly avoiding being crushed.

"Is this all you have?" Gilgamesh taunted, rising to his full height. He slashed at a branch that swung toward him, the blade severing it cleanly. The branch fell with a resounding crash, but Humbaba was already advancing, his enormous hand reaching for Gilgamesh.

Enkidu leapt onto Humbaba's arm, his club raised high. With a cry of raw power, he brought the weapon down on Humbaba's knotted skin, the impact resounding like a drumbeat. Humbaba bellowed in pain, shaking his arm violently to dislodge the wild man. Enkidu held on, his muscles straining, as he climbed higher, aiming for the guardian's neck.

Gilgamesh seized the moment, charging forward with his sword. Humbaba turned just in time, his massive hand swiping at the king. Gilgamesh ducked beneath the blow, driving his blade into Humbaba's side. The guardian roared, the sound echoing through the forest, as golden sap, thick and viscous, spilled from the wound.

"You cannot defeat me!" Humbaba thundered, his voice a mix of rage and desperation. "I am eternal! The forest and I are one!"

The trees around them seemed to respond to his words. Roots burst from the ground, thicker and more aggressive than before, their movements wild and erratic. Branches swung down with relentless force, splintering the earth and scattering debris. The forest itself seemed to scream in anguish, its energy focused entirely on the two intruders.

Gilgamesh and Enkidu fought with a unity born of their bond. Where one faltered, the other stepped in. Enkidu smashed through a root that lunged for Gilgamesh, while the king struck down a branch that threatened to crush Enkidu. Their movements were a dance of survival, their strength and determination the only things keeping them from being overwhelmed.

But even they began to tire. Gilgamesh's arms ached from the repeated strikes of his sword, his muscles burning with exertion. Enkidu's breath came in ragged gasps, his club heavy in his hands. Humbaba, though wounded, seemed to draw strength from the forest itself, his wounds closing as quickly as they were made.

"We need an opening!" Gilgamesh shouted, his voice desperate. "Enkidu, can you hold him?"

Enkidu nodded, his jaw set in grim determination. "I'll do more than hold him."

With a primal roar, Enkidu leapt onto Humbaba's back, his powerful arms wrapping around the guardian's thick neck. Humbaba thrashed and roared, his massive limbs tearing through the forest as he tried to dislodge the wild man. "Now, Gilgamesh!" Enkidu shouted, his voice straining with effort. "End this!"

Gilgamesh raised his sword high, its edge gleaming with a light that seemed to come from within him. He charged, his footsteps steady despite the chaos around him. With a mighty cry, he plunged the blade deep into Humbaba's chest, the weapon sinking through bark and sinew to find the core of the guardian's life force.

Humbaba froze, his eyes wide with shock and pain. A final roar erupted from his throat, a sound so loud and mournful that it seemed to shake the heavens. The forest stilled, its movements ceasing as Humbaba's massive body collapsed to the ground. The guardian lay motionless, his molten eyes dimming as the light of his life faded.

The forest, now silent, seemed to breathe a sigh of relief. The oppressive energy lifted, replaced by a stillness that felt almost sacred. Gilgamesh and Enkidu stood over Humbaba's fallen form, their bodies battered and bloodied, their breaths heavy. They exchanged a glance, their bond stronger than ever in the wake of their shared triumph.

"The gods decreed this," Gilgamesh said, his voice quiet but resolute. "And we have fulfilled their will."

Enkidu nodded, his expression solemn. "The forest will remember this day, as will we."

Chapter 9:

THE BRILLIANCE OF SHAMASH

The Cedar Forest was quiet, too quiet. The usual hum of life, from the rustling leaves to the distant chatter of unseen creatures, had fallen into an eerie stillness. Gilgamesh and Enkidu sat beside a small fire, the glow casting flickering shadows on their faces. They were weary, their bodies bruised and battered from the battle with Humbaba, but their minds were restless.

The severed head of the forest guardian lay nearby, its monstrous features frozen in a grimace of defiance. The weight of their victory hung heavy between them, not as a shared triumph but as a burden they both felt keenly.

Gilgamesh broke the silence first, his voice low and contemplative. "The forest feels… emptier," he said, gazing at the towering trees that surrounded them. "As if it grieves for what we've done."

Enkidu, sitting cross-legged and staring into the flames, nodded slowly. "Humbaba was not just a guardian; he was the soul of this place. Without him, the forest feels like a body without a heart. It will die."

Their conversation was interrupted by a sudden shift in the air. The fire flickered wildly, casting erratic shadows along the trees, as a warm, golden light began to suffuse the clearing. A low hum vibrated through the earth, a resonance that seemed to pulse in time with the very heart of the world. The oppressive stillness lifted, replaced by a force both immense and ancient.

Gilgamesh and Enkidu tensed, their instincts honed by battles against both mortal and divine foes. Their hands moved instinctively to their weapons, but before they could draw, the golden light thickened, folding in upon itself, swirling like molten metal. The heat intensified, not with the searing bite of flames, but with the embracing warmth of the sun at its zenith.

Then, from within the radiance, a figure emerged who was tall and resplendent, his form shimmering with celestial fire. His robe was woven from light itself, shifting between hues of dawn and dusk, and upon his brow shone a great, unblinking eye, the all-seeing emblem of justice. His presence was neither harsh nor cruel, but it bore the weight of absolute truth, a force that could not be denied.

Gilgamesh and Enkidu stood frozen as Shamash, the sun god, stepped forward. His eyes, twin orbs of burning gold, held the knowledge of ages, piercing through flesh and bone to the very core of the soul. There was no escaping his gaze, It was one where he saw all, knew all. Yet his voice, when he finally spoke, was a paradox of power and kindness, rolling over them like a river of sunlight breaking through the clouds.

"Gilgamesh, Enkidu," Shamash said, his tone resonating with divine authority. "You have walked a path of ambition and courage, but you have also trespassed upon sacred ground. Humbaba's death was a test, one I helped you to pass, though you knew it not."

Gilgamesh stepped forward, his voice steady despite the awe that filled him. "Shamash, great god of the sun, why would you aid us? Humbaba was the guardian of this place, placed here by the will of Enlil. Why did you not stand against us?"

Shamash's expression softened, his light dimming slightly as he regarded the two men. "The gods are not of one mind, Gilgamesh," he said. "Enlil saw Humbaba as a protector of sacred order, but I saw him as a force of stagnation, a barrier to your growth. I chose to aid you because your strength and determination have the potential to shape the world, to inspire greatness."

Enkidu, his wild mane catching the light, frowned. "You speak of aiding us, but we fought Humbaba with our own strength. What aid did you provide?"

Shamash's eyes glimmered with a knowing light. "I shielded you from the full wrath of the forest. The roots that sought to entangle you, the shadows that reached to blind you, they would have killed you both if it were not for my blessing. But my intervention does not end there. Humbaba's legacy remains, and his sons will not let his death go unchallenged."

At these words, a rustling sound emerged from the depths of the forest. The ground trembled faintly, and the air grew colder. Seven shapes emerged from the shadows, their forms monstrous and twisted, like smaller echoes of Humbaba. Each bore his fiery eyes and bark-like skin, but their movements were faster, more erratic. These were his sons, born of the forest's rage, and they had come for vengeance.

Gilgamesh and Enkidu readied their weapons, their exhaustion forgotten in the face of this new threat. But Shamash raised a hand, his radiant light flaring brighter. "Rest, mortals. This is not your fight."

One of Humbaba's sons lunged toward Shamash, its claws extended, but the god turned his gaze upon it, and the creature disintegrated into ash. Another leapt from the shadows, its bark-like hide bristling with spikes, but Shamash raised a hand, and it froze midair, suspended by an unseen force. With a flick of his wrist, Shamash sent it hurtling into the earth, where it shattered like stone.

The battle was a spectacle of divine power. Shamash moved with an elegance and ferocity that left Gilgamesh and Enkidu awestruck. The ground beneath them glowed with his radiance, and the forest seemed to bend to his will. The remaining sons of

Humbaba, though fierce, were no match for the god. One by one, they fell, their roars of defiance fading into the stillness of the night.

When the last of Humbaba's sons was reduced to ash, Shamash turned back to the two men. His light dimmed slightly, his divine aura settling into a quieter intensity. "Your path is now clear," he said. "But remember, Gilgamesh and Enkidu, the gods watch your every step. This victory comes at a cost, one that will reveal itself in time."

Gilgamesh bowed his head, his voice quiet but resolute. "Thank you, Shamash. Without your aid, we would not have survived. We will honor your guidance."

Shamash nodded, his gaze lingering on them for a moment before he began to fade, his form dissolving into the golden light of the dawn. "Take from the forest what you need, but leave its heart intact. Balance must be preserved, even in victory."

As the god disappeared, the forest returned to its uneasy quiet. Gilgamesh and Enkidu stood in silence for a moment, the weight of Shamash's words heavy upon them. Then, Gilgamesh turned to Enkidu, his expression thoughtful.

"We will take the sacred wood," he said. "The Cedar Forest will honor its guardian in the halls of Uruk. We will build a great entrance to the temple of Enlil, a testament to our strength and the power of the gods."

Enkidu hesitated, his gaze drifting toward the towering trees. "We have already taken much," he said softly. "To take more feels… wrong."

Gilgamesh placed a hand on his shoulder. "We will not take it all. Only enough to build something worthy of the gods, something that will endure. It will be our way of honoring what we have done here."

Reluctantly, Enkidu nodded. Together, they worked to fell the great trees, their hands steady despite their exhaustion. They fashioned a massive raft from the sacred wood. As they prepared to depart, the forest seemed to watch them, its presence both somber and resigned.

When the raft was complete, they pushed it into the river, the sacred wood carrying them toward Uruk. The journey home was quiet, their minds heavy with the memory of Shamash's intervention and the battle that had nearly claimed their lives. Yet beneath the weight of their thoughts, a spark of determination burned. They had faced the wrath of the gods and survived, and now they would carry the legacy of the Cedar Forest back to their city.

Chapter 10:

THE WRATH OF HUMBABA

The sun hung low on the horizon as Gilgamesh and Enkidu emerged from the Cedar Forest, their silhouettes stark against the golden light. Leaving the forest behind, they brought the raft to the shore. Between them, they carried the severed head of Humbaba, its monstrous features frozen in a grimace of fury and defiance. The air around them was heavy, the silence oppressive as though the forest itself mourned its fallen guardian. Though they had emerged victorious, each step away from the forest felt like a betrayal of something greater, a wound carved into the heart of the natural world.

The head was no simple trophy. Its weight seemed to grow with every mile, not just from its monstrous size but from the burden of their actions. Gilgamesh walked with his usual resolute stride, but even he felt the gravity of what they had done. His chest swelled with pride, yet a flicker of unease lingered. Enkidu, by contrast, carried the head with a far heavier heart. His wild mane clung to his sweat-soaked skin, and his gaze rarely left the horizon ahead, as if he dared not look back.

The silence between them was uncharacteristic. Their bond, forged in battle and deepened through shared ambition, now bore the strain of an unspoken tension. The journey back to Uruk stretched long and slow, each step reminding them of the fight they had endured and the guardian they had slain.

When they reached the gates of Uruk, the city erupted in celebration. Word of their triumph had already spread, and the streets were alive with jubilant cries. Children ran ahead, pointing in amazement at the severed head, while priests lined the thoroughfare, chanting blessings to the gods. Citizens threw flowers at their feet, their cheers echoing through the city walls. Drums pounded in rhythmic celebration, their beats mingling with the hum of ecstatic voices.

Gilgamesh held his head high, acknowledging the people with a nod of pride. He carried himself as the hero he believed himself to be, the king who had faced a god's fury and returned victorious. Enkidu, however, walked with his shoulders slumped, his gaze fixed on the cobbled streets. His grip on the head tightened as though it anchored him to the weight of his guilt.

As the procession reached the central square, the sky darkened unnaturally. The golden glow of sunset faded into a pall of heavy clouds, their edges tinged with crimson. A cold wind swept through the streets, silencing the cheers and replacing them with uneasy murmurs. The air itself seemed to still, thick with an otherworldly tension.

Gilgamesh sensed the change and raised his hand, his voice cutting through the growing unease. "People of Uruk, do not fear. The gods have seen our victory, and they will honor our courage!"

His words hung in the air, but they were answered by a deafening clap of thunder. The ground trembled, and the heavens split with a voice that seemed to carry the weight of eternity. It rolled across the city like a storm, layering fury and sorrow in every syllable.

"Gilgamesh! Enkidu!" the voice boomed, reverberating through the very stones of Uruk. "You have defied the will of the gods and slain Humbaba, the guardian of the sacred Cedar Forest. You have stolen life that was not yours to take, and for this, you will pay dearly."

The people fell to their knees, their faces pale with terror as they clutched one another for comfort. Gilgamesh and Enkidu stood frozen, the weight of divine judgment pressing against them. Gilgamesh clenched his fists, his jaw tightening as he steeled himself against the storm of condemnation.

"We sought only to test the limits of our strength!" Gilgamesh shouted to the heavens, his voice defiant. "Humbaba was a guardian, yes, but we are mortals striving to carve our place in the world. Is it a crime to seek greatness?"

The voice thundered again, colder and more resolute. "You have disrupted the balance. For your hubris, the gods shall demand their price."

A flash of lightning split the sky, illuminating the square in blinding brilliance. Torrential rain began to fall, cold and heavy, extinguishing the celebratory fires and drenching the streets. The storm raged like a living thing, the winds howling with the voices of lamentation. Through it all, the city shivered, its people huddled together in terrified silence.

The storm passed as quickly as it had come, leaving the city soaked and subdued. The streets were eerily quiet, the joyous cries of celebration replaced by whispers of dread. Gilgamesh and Enkidu carried Humbaba's head to the temple, laying it before the altar in a solemn act of tribute. The priests performed their rites with desperate fervor, their chants pleading for mercy, but the air remained heavy with foreboding.

In the days that followed, Uruk wore the shadow of divine judgment like a shroud. Though no further storms came, the people moved with a subdued caution, their movements hushed as though the gods themselves watched their every step. Gilgamesh buried himself in the affairs of the city, his every action carried out with a determination to distract himself from the storm's warning. But Enkidu could not escape his guilt.

Each night, Enkidu dreamed of the Cedar Forest. He would

speak of them with Gilgamesh every morning. In his dreams, its towering trees stood withered and lifeless, their once vibrant canopies reduced to ash. The streams ran dry, their beds cracked and barren. And always, he heard Humbaba's voice. It was a low, mournful cry that echoed through the desolation.

One evening, as the stars glittered above the palace courtyard, Enkidu spoke more in depth of his torment. "I see his face in my dreams," he said, his voice barely above a whisper. "The forest burns in my mind, its life extinguished. I feel his death like a wound in my soul."

Gilgamesh turned to him, his expression troubled. Though he had not spoken of it, the warning from the gods weighed heavily on him as well. Yet his pride refused to let him surrender to fear. "Humbaba was a guardian, yes, but he was also a test. The gods gave us strength to face such trials. They cannot fault us for fulfilling the destiny they placed before us."

Enkidu shook his head, his gaze distant. "Destiny does not absolve us. Humbaba was not just a beast to be conquered. He was a living part of the forest, its protector, its spirit. We have taken more than a life, Gilgamesh. We have wounded the world."

Gilgamesh placed a hand on Enkidu's shoulder, his grip firm. "If the gods wished to stop us, they would have. Whatever price they demand, we will face it together. Do not let guilt cloud your heart, Enkidu. We are stronger than their judgment."

Enkidu nodded, but his eyes remained shadowed. "Together," he said, though the word carried a note of sorrow that Gilgamesh could not ignore.

Chapter 11:

TO DENY A GODDESS

The evening sun cast its final rays over Uruk, painting the city in hues of gold and amber. The bustle of the day faded into a calm hush as the people returned to their homes, the sounds of laughter and conversation giving way to the occasional bark of a dog or the rustle of leaves carried on a gentle breeze. Within the palace courtyard, Gilgamesh sat alone, his thoughts heavy and his expression distant. The weight of his kingship and the recent trials with Humbaba lingered in his mind, casting a shadow over his usual confidence.

His thoughts were interrupted by a commotion at the palace gates. The sound of voices raised in awe and fear carried through the courtyard, accompanied by the faint shimmer of a presence that made the air around him feel charged. He looked up, his sharp gaze narrowing as the figure of a goddess emerged from the gates, her very presence causing even the most seasoned guards to fall to their knees.

Ishtar.

She descended upon the palace like a storm wrapped in silk. Her robes shimmered with celestial light, adorned with jewels that caught the fading sun and reflected it in dazzling hues. Her beauty was unparalleled, her movements deliberate and predatory, each step exuding power and command. The air around her seemed to

59

shimmer, and even the wind carried her intoxicating fragrance.

Gilgamesh rose slowly, his gaze steady but wary. He had encountered the gods before, and he knew their beauty often concealed dangerous intent. Ishtar's radiant smile drew his attention, but her eyes, cold and calculating, betrayed the purpose of her visit.

"Gilgamesh," she said, her voice smooth and melodic, wrapping around him like silk. "King of Uruk, whose fame reaches even the halls of the gods. I have come to see the man whose deeds echo through the heavens."

Gilgamesh inclined his head respectfully, though his expression remained guarded. "Goddess Ishtar, your presence honors this city," he said, his voice calm. "What brings you to Uruk?"

Ishtar stepped closer, her gaze locking onto his with an intensity that made the air between them feel electric. "I have heard of your strength, your courage, and your unmatched victories," she said. "I have seen kings and warriors, but none as great as you, Gilgamesh. I offer you my love and my hand in marriage. Together, we would be invincible. With my divine power and your strength, we could rule the world."

Her words hung in the air, seductive and deliberate, each syllable a promise of glory and power. Any mortal man would have crumbled beneath the weight of her offer, overcome by the allure of ruling alongside a goddess. But Gilgamesh was no ordinary man. He had faced gods before, walked paths no other dared tread, and he recognized the danger veiled beneath her offer.

"Goddess," he began, his voice steady and measured, "your offer flatters me. But I must refuse."

For the first time, a flicker of irritation crossed Ishtar's flawless face. "Refuse?" she repeated, her tone sharp despite its melodic quality. "You refuse the queen of heaven? The goddess of love and war?"

Gilgamesh's gaze did not falter. "I refuse because I know the fate of those who have accepted your love," he said. "Kings brought low, warriors left broken, their greatness consumed by your whims. Your love is a storm, Ishtar. It is beautiful and destructive. I will not be swept away."

Her smile vanished, replaced by an icy glare that seemed to pierce through him. "You insult me, mortal," she said, her voice rising, the air around her charged with an impending storm. "You, a king, dare to defy the queen of heaven?"

"I do," Gilgamesh replied, his tone unwavering. "Because I will not sacrifice my people or my own honor for a fleeting promise of power."

Ishtar's fury erupted like lightning. The air around her crackled, her radiant beauty now edged with wrath. "You will regret this insult, Gilgamesh," she hissed, her voice a venomous whisper. "No man rejects Ishtar and escapes unscathed."

With a final glare, she raised her hand, and a gust of wind tore through the courtyard, extinguishing the torches and scattering leaves. When the wind subsided, she was gone, leaving behind only the echo of her fury and the acrid scent of scorched air.

Gilgamesh stood in the silence of the courtyard, his chest heaving. Though he would not admit it, Ishtar's wrath unnerved him. He had faced the fury of Humbaba and the judgment of the gods, but this felt different. The goddess's words echoed in his mind, their weight settling like a shadow over his thoughts.

That night, he sought Enkidu. The wild man sat by the fire in one of the palace chambers, his rugged features softened by the flickering light. When Gilgamesh entered, Enkidu looked up, his sharp gaze immediately noticing the tension in the king's posture.

"What troubles you?" Enkidu asked, his voice calm but concerned.

Gilgamesh sat beside him, the firelight dancing across his face. "Ishtar," he said, the single word heavy with meaning. He recounted the encounter, his refusal, and the goddess's wrath. As he spoke, Enkidu listened intently, his expression growing darker with each word.

"She will not forgive this," Enkidu said when Gilgamesh finished. "Her pride is as vast as her power. Her vengeance will come, and it will not be subtle."

Gilgamesh nodded, his jaw tightening. "I do not fear her," he said, though a trace of unease crept into his voice. "But I fear what her wrath may mean for Uruk. It is not just me she seeks to punish."

Enkidu placed a hand on his shoulder, his grip firm. "Whatever she brings, we will face it together," he said. "We have stood against gods before, and we will stand against her. I must ask, however, why you would refuse Ishtar?"

Gilgamesh looked at the fire, knowing the answer in his heart. "You."

The fire crackled between them, its warmth a small comfort against the chill of Ishtar's looming vengeance. In that moment, the bond between them felt unbreakable, their loyalty and love a shield against even the fury of a goddess. Yet, in the quiet of the night, both men understood that their defiance of Ishtar would set in motion events that neither could fully anticipate.

Together, they waited, knowing that the storm was only beginning to gather.

Chapter 12

DREAMS OF DESTRUCTIONS

The air in Uruk hung heavy, a weight that pressed against the city like an unseen hand. The tension was palpable, stretching across the walls and winding through the streets. Dark clouds churned in the skies above, their ominous shapes shifting and swirling as if bearing witness to the gods' anger. The people whispered of Ishtar's vengeance, their voices low and trembling. The goddess's wrath had not abated, and the city braced for the storm that would surely follow.

Gilgamesh moved through the palace halls, his steps steady but his thoughts uneasy. His rejection of Ishtar's offer had been an act of defiance, born of his pride and his determination to remain unbound by any but Enkidu. But now, the consequences of that choice loomed, their shape unknown but their presence undeniable. Even Gilgamesh, for all his strength and confidence, felt the weight of divine retribution gathering on the horizon.

Enkidu sensed it too. He stood on the palace balcony, his sharp eyes scanning the darkened skies, his instincts honed by years in the wilderness whispering of danger. When Gilgamesh joined him, they exchanged no words at first, their bond speaking louder than any conversation. Together, they gazed out over the city, their beloved Uruk bathed in a dim, muted light beneath the roiling heavens.

"They will send something," Enkidu said at last, his voice

steady but heavy with certainty. "Ishtar's pride will not allow her anger to fade. She will strike, and it will be swift and terrible."

Gilgamesh turned to him, his expression resolute. "Let her send what she will," he said. "We have faced the fury of gods and demons before. Together, we will endure this as well."

That night, as the city settled into uneasy slumber, Gilgamesh found no such peace. He lay restless in his chambers, his mind churning with thoughts of the goddess and the wrath she would surely unleash. When sleep finally claimed him, it brought no solace. It brought only a dream of foreboding.

In the dream, Gilgamesh stood not in Uruk but in a realm of swirling stars and endless skies. Before him, Ishtar loomed, her radiant beauty sharpened by an expression of fury. Her robes billowed like storm clouds, her eyes blazing with a fire that seemed to burn through him. She raised her arms, her voice echoing with divine authority.

"Father!" she cried, her voice carrying through the heavens. "Gilgamesh has insulted me, defied me, and rejected the love of the queen of heaven. He must be punished!"

From the swirling void emerged Anu, her father, the god of the sky. His form was vast and ethereal, his presence commanding. His expression was one of calm yet unyielding authority. "Ishtar," he said, his voice measured but firm. "Your pride blinds you. Gilgamesh is mortal. His refusal does not warrant divine vengeance."

Ishtar's face twisted with rage. "You would defend him? You would let this insult stand?" she demanded, her voice rising like the roar of a tempest. "If you will not act, I will raise the dead! They will outnumber the living and devour them, dragging the world into chaos. My screams will echo from the heavens to the earth until the gods themselves tremble."

Her words carried a terrible weight, and Gilgamesh felt the air around him thicken with the threat of her wrath. Anu's eyes narrowed, his tone hardening. "If I give you the Bull of Heaven, the people of Uruk will face seven years of famine. Is this what you wish? To destroy the balance for the sake of your pride?"

"I will provide for them," Ishtar insisted, her voice fierce. "For seven years, I will fill their storehouses, and they will not suffer. Grant me the Bull of Heaven, Father, or I will bring ruin upon the mortal world."

Anu's gaze bore into hers for a long moment, the stars seeming to pause in their celestial dance. Finally, he nodded, his expression grave. "So be it. Take the Bull of Heaven, but know this, Ishtar, your actions will have consequences, even for the gods."

With a wave of his hand, the dream shifted. Gilgamesh saw Ishtar leading the Bull of Heaven, a creature of terrifying size and power. Its eyes burned with an unnatural fire, its breath steaming like smoke from a volcano. The ground cracked beneath its hooves as it descended toward Uruk, its presence a harbinger of destruction.

Gilgamesh awoke with a start, his chest heaving as though he had run for miles. The room was still and dark, but the weight of the dream lingered like a shroud. He rose from his bed, his movements deliberate as he made his way to the courtyard where Enkidu often found solace beneath the stars.

He found his companion seated on the cool stone, his posture relaxed but his expression alert. Enkidu looked up as Gilgamesh approached, his sharp eyes narrowing slightly at the tension radiating from the king.

"What is it?" Enkidu asked, his voice low but steady.

Gilgamesh sat beside him, his gaze fixed on the heavens. "I dreamt of Ishtar," he said, the words heavy with the truth of divine revelation. He recounted the vision in detail, his voice calm but edged with unease. Enkidu listened intently, his expression darkening with every word.

"The Bull of Heaven," Enkidu said when Gilgamesh finished.

"It is no ordinary beast. It is destruction given form, sent to lay waste to all in its path. If it comes to Uruk, the city will not survive."

Gilgamesh nodded, his jaw tightening. "Then we will stop it before it destroys what we have built," he said. "We have faced the fury of gods before, Enkidu. This will be no different."

As the first light of dawn crept over the horizon, the two men sat in silence, their bond unshaken despite the weight of what lay ahead. The shadow of Ishtar's vengeance loomed large, but they were resolute. Uruk was their city, their people, and they would fight to protect it, even against the might of the gods.

Chapter 13:

THE BULL OF HEAVEN

The earth beneath Uruk trembled, its quaking a harbinger of the divine wrath descending upon the city. Gilgamesh and Enkidu stood on the palace balcony, their eyes scanning the darkened skies as thunder rumbled like the roar of a distant beast. The people below moved in a panic, their cries rising as the ground shuddered beneath them. The noise grew louder and louder, a pounding, relentless and rhythmic, like a drumbeat from the heavens. It was the sound of hooves.

The Bull of Heaven arrived with the force of a god's fury. From the roiling clouds above, it descended in a flash of light, landing in the city square with an impact that split the earth and sent shockwaves rippling outward. The ground cracked beneath its massive hooves, and the air around it shimmered with an unbearable heat. The beast was immense, its size dwarfing any mortal creature. Its hide was a dark, unnatural black, gleaming as though forged from molten metal, and its fiery eyes blazed with unrelenting malice. Steam rose from its nostrils, and with each breath it exhaled, the very air seemed to sear and burn.

The Bull let out a bellow that shook the heavens, a sound so loud it left the people clutching their ears in agony. The city froze in terror, its people paralyzed as the creature charged forward. Its hooves struck the ground with the force of thunder, crushing stones into dust. Its massive horns, curved like crescents of polished obsidian, tore through the air as it plowed through homes and markets, leaving ruin in its wake.

From their vantage point, Gilgamesh and Enkidu watched as the city descended into chaos. Fires erupted where the Bull's breath ignited hay and thatch. Buildings crumbled as its sheer bulk crashed through them. The screams of the people filled the air, their terror a sharp counterpoint to the Bull's enraged bellows. Gilgamesh gripped the hilt of his sword, his jaw set in grim determination.

"This is Ishtar's vengeance," he said, his voice tight with anger. "She sends this beast to destroy all I have built because I dared to defy her."

Enkidu's sharp eyes stayed fixed on the creature, his instincts honed by years in the wild. "If we do not act, Uruk will fall," he said. "We cannot let that happen."

Gilgamesh nodded, his resolve firm. "Then we will face it together, as we have faced every challenge."

The two descended from the palace into the chaos of the streets. People fled in every direction, their fear rendering them blind to the path ahead. Gilgamesh and Enkidu moved with purpose, their presence cutting through the panic like a beacon of hope. The citizens who saw them paused, their terror giving way to a flicker of belief that their king and his companion could save them.

In the central square, the Bull of Heaven stood surrounded by destruction. Its hooves dug deep gouges into the earth, its fiery gaze scanning the city for more to destroy. When it caught sight of Gilgamesh and Enkidu, it let out another deafening roar, its massive body lowering in preparation to charge.

"Beast of the heavens!" Gilgamesh shouted, his voice cutting through the chaos. "You have brought ruin to my city, but your rampage ends now. Face me!"

The Bull responded with a snort that sent sparks flying. It

pawed the ground, the muscles in its massive frame rippling as it lunged forward, its horns aimed directly at Gilgamesh. The king leapt aside at the last moment, his movements precise and measured. The Bull's charge sent a shockwave through the ground, toppling what remained of a nearby structure.

Enkidu darted in from the side, his strength focused on the creature's legs. With a roar, he struck the Bull's hind leg with his club, the impact reverberating through its massive form. The beast bellowed in rage, twisting to face him, its horns swinging in a deadly arc. Enkidu narrowly avoided the blow, rolling to safety as Gilgamesh charged from the other side.

The Bull of Heaven roared, its cry splitting the skies and shaking the very foundations of Uruk. The sound was deafening, a primal declaration of rage that seemed to reverberate in the bones of everyone who heard it. The beast's massive form towered above the city, its dark hide shimmering as though forged from molten iron. Fire flared from its nostrils, each breath sending waves of heat that scorched the air and blackened the stone beneath its hooves. Its crescent-shaped horns glinted menacingly, sharp enough to tear through steel, and its fiery eyes burned with the wrath of the gods.

Gilgamesh and Enkidu faced the creature from the shattered steps of a ruined temple, their weapons gleaming in the dim light of the darkened sky. Around them, Uruk lay in ruins. Entire sections of the city had been flattened by the bull's rampage. Homes were reduced to rubble, and marketplaces that were once alive with the hum of trade were now nothing but scorched earth. Smoke rose in thick plumes from fires ignited by the bull's breath, the acrid stench of destruction clinging to the air.

The Bull of Heaven stamped its hooves, each impact sending tremors through the ground and splintering the stone beneath it. Its fiery gaze locked onto Gilgamesh, and it let out another ear-splitting bellow, its massive muscles coiling as it prepared to charge.

"Here it comes!" Gilgamesh shouted, his voice cutting through the chaos. He raised his bronze sword, its edge glinting even in the smoky haze. "Enkidu, stay close to its legs! We need to slow it down!"

Enkidu nodded, his expression fierce and focused. "I'll keep it distracted. Strike when you see an opening!"

The bull charged, its massive frame moving with a speed that defied its size. Its hooves tore through the ground, sending shards of stone flying in all directions. Gilgamesh dodged to the side at the last moment, the bull's horns missing him by mere inches. The creature's momentum carried it forward, smashing through what remained of a stone wall and leaving a gaping hole in its wake.

Enkidu seized the opportunity, darting toward the bull's hind legs. With a roar, he swung his club with all his might, the weapon striking the creature's leg with a thunderous crack. The bull bellowed in pain, its fiery eyes flashing as it turned to face him. It lashed out with a kick, its massive hoof grazing Enkidu and sending him sprawling across the ground.

Gilgamesh rushed in, his sword aimed at the bull's exposed side. He struck true, the blade biting deep into the creature's flank. Golden ichor, thick and steaming, spilled from the wound, hissing as it hit the ground. The bull roared again, this time in rage, and swung its massive horns in a deadly arc. Gilgamesh leapt back, narrowly avoiding the strike, but the force of the blow sent a shockwave through the air, knocking him off balance.

The bull's eyes burned with renewed fury, and it reared onto its hind legs, its massive frame looming like a dark mountain against the smoky sky. It brought its front hooves crashing down, the impact creating a shockwave that radiated outward, toppling nearby structures and sending both men sprawling.

"It's too strong!" Enkidu shouted, his voice strained as he scrambled to his feet. "We need to weaken it further!"

Gilgamesh wiped sweat and dirt from his brow, his chest heaving as he stared at the beast. His mind raced, calculating their next move. "The legs!" he called. "If we can take out its legs, it won't be able to move as quickly. Focus your attacks there!"

The two men charged together, their movements coordinated and deliberate. Enkidu went low, his club striking at the bull's knees with relentless force. Gilgamesh leapt onto the creature's side, his sword slashing at its flank in rapid strikes. The beast thrashed wildly, its movements shaking the ground as it tried to dislodge its attackers.

The bull let out a guttural roar and twisted its massive body, throwing Gilgamesh off its side. The king landed hard, his sword clattering to the ground. The bull turned its fiery gaze on him, its horns lowering as it prepared to charge. But before it could move, Enkidu sprang onto its back, his powerful arms wrapping around its neck. The bull bucked and thrashed, its movements violent and chaotic, but Enkidu held on with an iron grip.

"Now, Gilgamesh!" Enkidu shouted, his voice strained but unwavering. "Take it down!"

Gilgamesh seized his sword and rose to his feet, his eyes blazing with determination. With a roar of his own, he surged forward, his blade gleaming as he drove it into the bull's chest with all his strength. The creature let out an ear-splitting bellow, its fiery eyes dimming as its massive body shuddered. Gilgamesh twisted the blade, driving it deeper, and the bull collapsed to the ground, its enormous frame sending up a cloud of dust and debris.

The silence that followed was profound, broken only by the crackle of distant fires and the ragged breaths of the two warriors. Gilgamesh and Enkidu stood over the fallen beast, their bodies battered and bloodied but victorious. The Bull of Heaven lay still, its dark hide steaming as its lifeblood pooled beneath it.

Chapter 14:

THE HEART OF THE BEAST

The dust from the battle hung thick in the air, settling over Uruk like a heavy shroud. The city, battered and broken, bore the scars of the Bull of Heaven's rampage. In the center of the square, the colossal beast lay motionless, its fiery eyes extinguished, its once-mighty horns glinting dully in the fading light. The creature, a manifestation of Ishtar's wrath, had brought destruction to Uruk, but it had been defeated. The great Bull of Heaven had been felled by the combined might of Gilgamesh and Enkidu. Yet, even in triumph, the city was quiet, its people hesitant to breathe freely in the shadow of such divine vengeance.

Gilgamesh stood tall, his sword still slick with the blood of the beast, his chest heaving with the exertion of battle. Beside him, Enkidu remained at the ready, his club in hand, his wild mane damp with sweat and dusted with the remnants of their struggle. Together, they were a sight to behold, two men who had done the impossible and stared down the fury of the gods. The silence of the square was punctuated only by the faint crackle of distant fires, the groan of crumbling buildings, and the muffled cries of the wounded.

Then, slowly, the people of Uruk began to emerge from the wreckage. First, a few cautious figures stepped into the light, their faces etched with fear and disbelief. Soon, more joined them, until a crowd gathered, their eyes wide as they took in the sight of the fallen Bull and the two warriors who had brought it down. Whispers spread like wildfire, their voices trembling as they spoke the names of their king and his companion. Gilgamesh. Enkidu. The men who had slain the Bull of Heaven.

The silence broke with a tentative cheer, a single voice raised in hope. It was quickly joined by another, and another, until the square erupted in celebration. The people surged forward, their fear melting into joy as they raised their voices in triumph. Women wept openly, clutching their children to their sides, while men raised their fists to the heavens, shouting the names of their heroes. The sound was deafening, a roar of relief and gratitude that reverberated through the broken city.

Gilgamesh lifted his sword high, his voice cutting through the cacophony with the clarity of a bell. "People of Uruk!" he called, his tone commanding but filled with pride. "The gods sent their fury to test us, to break us. But we have stood firm. We have triumphed over the Bull of Heaven! Today, Uruk remains unbroken, and our names will echo through eternity!"

The crowd erupted into fresh cheers, their voices a wave of hope and triumph that seemed to push back the darkness that hung over the city. But amidst the jubilation, Enkidu remained quiet. His gaze lingered on the fallen Bull, its lifeless body a stark reminder of the battle they had fought. The weight of their actions pressed heavily on him, and his brow furrowed with unease. He had fought bravely, as he always did, but this, this was different. To slay a creature of the gods was no small feat, but it was also no small crime.

Gilgamesh, ever attuned to his companion's moods, turned to him. "Enkidu," he said, his voice low enough that only the wild man could hear. "Why does this victory rest so uneasily on your shoulders?"

Enkidu did not answer immediately. His eyes remained fixed on the Bull's enormous body, its stillness almost unnatural in contrast to the chaos it had caused. "We have slain a divine creature," he said at last, his voice quiet but steady. "This was not merely a beast,

Gilgamesh. It was a weapon of the gods, sent by Ishtar herself. Killing it was an act of defiance, not just strength. The gods will not ignore this."

Gilgamesh placed a hand on his companion's shoulder, his grip firm but comforting. "We are not mere mortals, Enkidu," he said, his tone resolute. "The gods may test us, but they gave us the strength to face these trials. If they send their wrath again, we will meet it head-on, as we always have."

Enkidu met his gaze, his expression troubled but unwavering. "Strength alone will not shield us from the consequences of this, Gilgamesh. The gods are not so easily defied."

Before Gilgamesh could respond, the sky darkened, the sunlight fading as if swallowed by an unseen force. A chill wind swept through the square, carrying with it the faint, haunting sound of distant wailing. The crowd fell silent, their celebratory cries dying on their lips as a new presence made itself known. From the shadows of the temple ruins, Ishtar appeared.

The goddess's beauty was as radiant as ever, but her eyes burned with fury, their light rivaling the flames that still licked at the edges of the square. Her robes billowed around her, catching an unseen wind, and her presence commanded an immediate, reverent silence. The people of Uruk fell to their knees, their fear palpable as they dared not meet her gaze.

"Gilgamesh," Ishtar said, her voice echoing like thunder. "You have slain the Bull of Heaven, the weapon I sent to punish your arrogance. You, who dared to reject the queen of heaven, have committed an act of unforgivable defiance. Do you believe you can kill a creature of the gods and escape unscathed?"

Gilgamesh stepped forward, his shoulders squared and his chin held high. "Your vengeance brought ruin to my city and endangered my people," he said, his voice unwavering. "We acted not out of arrogance, but out of necessity. We defended Uruk, and we will continue to do so."

Ishtar's eyes narrowed, her fury palpable. "You speak of defense, but your actions reek of hubris. The gods will see your insolence punished."

Before she could say more, Enkidu, his own anger ignited by the goddess's words, strode forward. In a single, defiant motion, he bent down and grasped one of the massive hindquarters of the Bull. With a roar, he hurled it at Ishtar, the severed limb arcing through the air before landing with a sickening thud at her feet.

"If you seek vengeance, Ishtar," Enkidu growled, his voice filled with scorn, "then face us yourself. Do not hide behind your divine beasts."

The crowd gasped, their collective horror evident in the sharp intake of breath that swept through the square. Ishtar's face twisted with rage, her radiant beauty contorted into something terrible. "You will regret this, Enkidu," she spat, her voice venomous. "Your days are numbered."

With a final, searing glare, she vanished, her form dissolving into the air. The oppressive silence that followed was almost unbearable, the weight of her parting words hanging heavily over the square.

Gilgamesh turned to Enkidu, his expression a mixture of admiration and concern. "You've angered her further," he said, his voice laced with both respect and unease.

"She deserves no less," Enkidu replied, though his tone betrayed the faintest trace of doubt.

As the people of Uruk began to murmur and stir, Gilgamesh placed a hand on Enkidu's shoulder, their bond unshaken even in the face of divine wrath. Together, they lifted the Bull's massive heart, its divine essence still pulsing faintly, and carried it to the temple of Shamash. There, they offered it as a tribute, their prayers rising with the smoke of incense. For all their defiance, they sought the favor of the sun god, the one deity who had stood with them before.

The aftermath of the Bull's death lingered in the city's air, a mixture of triumph and foreboding. Gilgamesh and Enkidu had faced the wrath of the heavens and emerged victorious, but they both knew that this was only the beginning. The gods' judgment would come again, and the shadow of their defiance would follow them, shaping the destiny that lay ahead.

Chapter 15:

A VOICE FROM THE SKY

That evening, Uruk erupted into celebration as it once again had reason to celebrate life. The city, still bearing the scars of its recent battle, shimmered with a defiant warmth. Fires burned bright in the streets, their glow pushing back the shadows of fear. The scent of roasted meat, spiced wine, and honeyed bread filled the air, mingling with the jubilant music of flutes, drums, and lyres. The people danced in the square, their voices rising in song as they toasted their king and his companion, the saviors of Uruk.

Gilgamesh and Enkidu moved through the throngs like living legends. Wherever they went, the crowd parted, cheers erupting as hands reached out to touch them. Gilgamesh accepted their praises with a steady gaze, his chin held high, but there was a heaviness in his eyes that only Enkidu could see. Enkidu, ever the wild spirit, smiled faintly and exchanged quiet words with the people, but even his usual vigor seemed muted. The weight of what they had done lingered over them like an unseen shadow.

At the heart of the celebration, a great feast was laid out in the palace courtyard. Platters of roasted lamb and fresh fruit lined the tables, and jugs of sweet wine flowed freely. The people of Uruk reveled, their laughter and song reverberating against the palace walls. For a time, it seemed as though the city's joy could banish the specter of divine judgment that hung over them.

But as the night deepened, a chill swept through Uruk, one that did not come from the cool desert air. The fires flickered and dimmed, their warm light replaced by an eerie, wavering glow. The music faltered, the musicians pausing as an unnatural stillness descended upon the city. The sky, once glittering with stars, darkened as though veiled by a vast and impenetrable shadow.

Then, from above, a voice boomed, its power shaking the earth beneath their feet. It was Enlil, his tone thunderous and unyielding. "Gilgamesh! Enkidu!" the voice roared, each syllable a hammer blow of divine authority. "You have slain the Bull of Heaven, defied the will of the gods, and disrupted the balance decreed by the heavens. For your arrogance, a price must be paid."

The crowds fell to their knees, trembling as the divine voice reverberated through the air. Fear rippled through them, their earlier jubilation extinguished like a candle snuffed out by the wind. Gilgamesh and Enkidu alone stood firm, their shoulders squared against the invisible weight of judgment. Gilgamesh stepped forward, his voice rising with defiance.

"We acted to protect our people!" he shouted, his tone steady despite the storm of fear around him. "If punishment is due, let it fall upon me! I am their king, and the responsibility is mine!"

Enlil's voice answered, as unrelenting as the wind and as cold as the night. "The price must be paid by the one who defies the natural order. Enkidu, created to balance Gilgamesh, you have joined him in his defiance. For this, your life shall be forfeit."

The words struck like a thunderclap, their finality settling over the city like an iron shroud. Enkidu's breath hitched, the weight of the decree pressing down on him with the force of mountains. Gilgamesh turned to him, his eyes blazing with fury and desperation.

"No!" he roared, his voice raw with emotion. "Take me instead! Enkidu is my equal. He does not deserve this!"

But the heavens did not answer. The voice of Enlil fell silent, and the oppressive shadow over Uruk began to recede. The stars returned to the sky, their light cold and distant, and the unnatural chill lifted. Yet, the silence that followed was more deafening than the voice of the god. The people remained kneeling, their faces pale with the realization of what had transpired.

Enkidu placed a hand on Gilgamesh's arm, his grip firm despite the sorrow in his eyes. "It is done," he said quietly, his voice steady but heavy. "The gods have spoken, and their will is absolute."

Gilgamesh's fists clenched at his sides, his body trembling with rage and grief. "I will not accept this," he said fiercely. "I will find a way to defy them. I will save you."

Enkidu smiled faintly, his expression softening as he gazed at his friend. "You are a great king, my dear friend," he said, his tone filled with both love and resignation. "But even kings cannot rewrite the will of the gods. If this is my fate, I will face it with honor."

The celebration had turned to mourning. The people who had cheered for their king and his companion now whispered prayers for mercy, their joy tempered by the cold certainty of divine wrath. The fires burned low, their light muted as the weight of the gods' judgment settled over Uruk.

Gilgamesh and Enkidu retreated to the palace, their bond unshaken but their hearts heavy with the knowledge that their time together was slipping away. They sat in the quiet of the grand hall, the flickering torchlight casting long shadows on the walls. Gilgamesh's mind raced, every fiber of his being rebelling against the inevitability of what was to come.

"I will not let this happen," he said, his voice barely above a whisper. "There must be a way to undo this."

Enkidu watched him, his expression calm but sorrowful. "The gods do not bargain, Gilgamesh," he said gently. "They have spoken. My life will be the price of our defiance."

Gilgamesh's eyes burned with unshed tears, his jaw tightening as he stared at his friend. "I refuse to lose you, Enkidu. You are more than my companion. You are my equal, the one I am fated to be with. I cannot, will not, let the gods take you from me."

Enkidu leaned forward, placing a hand over Gilgamesh's clenched fist. "If I must go, then let my life serve as a reminder of what we have achieved together. Do not let grief consume you, Gilgamesh. Your destiny is greater than this moment."

The weight of Enkidu's words settled over Gilgamesh like a mantle, heavy and unyielding. He closed his eyes, his breath shuddering as he fought to steady himself. "I will find a way," he said at last, his voice firm with determination. "If there is even the smallest chance, I will defy the gods again to save you. I need you."

Enkidu did not reply, his silence an acknowledgment of both Gilgamesh's resolve and the inevitability of his fate. Together, they sat in the quiet of the hall, their bond unspoken but unbreakable. Outside, the city of Uruk lay in uneasy silence, its people haunted by the events of the night and the shadow of divine retribution that loomed over them all.

Chapter 16

A COUNCIL OF NIGHTMARES

The shadows of the night were heavy in the grand hall of Uruk's palace, the flickering light of the torches casting restless patterns across the stone walls. Gilgamesh sat at the edge of Enkidu's bed, his face a mask of quiet worry. Enkidu's breaths were shallow, his chest rising and falling as he lay ensnared in a sleep that seemed anything but peaceful. His brow was furrowed, his powerful frame tense as if locked in battle with an unseen foe. Gilgamesh, for all his strength and resolve, felt powerless in the face of his friend's torment.

The dream had seized Enkidu as the night deepened. Gilgamesh had been awakened by his companion's muttered cries, his hands clenching the air as if grasping at phantoms. Now, the king waited, his heart heavy as he watched Enkidu wrestle with forces he could not see.

In the dream, Enkidu stood before the assembly of the gods. Their forms towered above him, radiant and terrible, their voices like the rumble of distant thunder. Enlil, stern and unyielding, presided over the council, his gaze fixed on Enkidu with a cold finality. Shamash, the sun god, stood at his side, his face a mixture of defiance and sorrow.

"Humbaba has fallen," Enlil intoned, his voice resonating through the dreamscape. "The guardian of the Cedar Forest, slain by mortal hands. The Bull of Heaven, sent to exact our judgment, has met the same fate. The balance has been broken. One of the offenders must pay the price."

Shamash stepped forward, his golden light shimmering with urgency. "Enlil," he said, his tone pleading, "these men acted not out of arrogance, but necessity. Humbaba and the Bull were forces of destruction. Their deaths were acts of protection, not defiance."

Enlil's gaze did not waver. "The gods are not to be defied, Shamash. Mortals must know their place. If we do not act, they will believe they are untouchable."

The assembly murmured their agreement, their celestial forms glowing with an unsettling intensity. Then Enlil spoke again, his voice cutting through the clamor. "Enkidu was created to temper Gilgamesh, to balance his ambition. Yet he has joined him in his defiance. It is Enkidu who will pay the price."

"No!" Shamash's voice rang out, filled with anguish. "Enkidu has brought balance to Gilgamesh. Without him, the king would be lost to his own recklessness. If you take him, you condemn not just a man but a kingdom."

But the gods were unmoved. The decree had been made. Enkidu felt the weight of their judgment settle over him, crushing and inescapable.

When Enkidu awoke, his cries shattered the quiet of the palace. Gilgamesh was at his side in an instant, gripping his shoulder with a strength that spoke of desperation. "Enkidu! What is it? Speak to me!"

Enkidu's eyes were wide and wild, his face pale and glistening with sweat. He stared at Gilgamesh as though seeing him for the first time, his voice trembling as he spoke. "The gods," he rasped. "They have decreed it. I am to die for what we have done."

Gilgamesh's breath caught, his heart hammering in his chest. "No," he said, his voice firm, as if sheer denial could rewrite the will of the gods. "This cannot be. We have faced their wrath and survived. We will find a way to defy them again."

Enkidu shook his head, his expression filled with a sorrow that cut deeper than any blade. "Their decree is final, Gilgamesh. Enlil himself has spoken. Shamash protested, but even he could not sway them."

As the weight of the dream's meaning settled over them, Enkidu's sorrow turned to anger. He pushed himself upright, his eyes blazing. "The door!" he spat, his voice filled with bitterness. "What use was the great door I carved for the temple of Enlil? It stands as a monument to the very gods who have condemned me. I curse it!"

Gilgamesh watched in silence, his throat tight as Enkidu's rage consumed him. Enkidu's hands clenched into fists, his fury spilling over. "And the trapper!" he snarled. "It was he who first saw me in the wild and sought to tame me. Without him, I would still roam free, untouched by the curse of the gods. I curse him and all his works!"

His voice broke as his anger gave way to despair. "And Shamhat," he said, his tone softer but no less anguished. "She fed me, clothed me, and brought me to this life of men. But it was her hand that led me from the wilderness, to this place, to this fate. I curse her, too."

At this, a warm light filled the chamber, and Shamash appeared before them. The sun god's form was radiant, his presence filling the room with a sense of calm. He looked upon Enkidu with a mixture of sorrow and compassion.

"Enkidu," Shamash said gently, his voice like the first rays of dawn, "do not let your grief turn to hatred. You curse Shamhat, yet it was she who showed you the ways of men, who brought you to Gilgamesh. Without her, you would never have known the bond you now share."

Enkidu's breath hitched, his gaze falling to the ground.

Shamash stepped closer, his light washing over him. "The gods may take your life, but they cannot take the legacy you leave behind. Gilgamesh will honor you, Enkidu. He will ensure that your name is remembered, that your deeds echo through the ages. And though grief will consume him, it will also drive him to greatness."

Enkidu closed his eyes, his body trembling as Shamash's words settled over him. Gilgamesh, his heart aching, reached out and gripped his friend's hand. "You will not be forgotten," he said, his voice thick with emotion. "I swear it, Enkidu. Your name will live on, and your memory will guide me. I will not let the gods erase you."

Shamash nodded, his gaze lingering on the two men. "The bond you share is rare, even among the gods. It is a light that will not be extinguished, no matter the darkness that comes."

As the sun god's presence faded, the room fell silent once more. Enkidu slumped back against the bed, his strength waning as the weight of his fate pressed down upon him. Gilgamesh remained at his side, his resolve hardening with each passing moment. He would not let this be the end. He would find a way to defy the gods, to challenge the very fabric of their will if it meant saving his friend.

Chapter 17:

AN ILL FATE

The room was heavy with silence, broken only by the sound of Enkidu's labored breathing. Gilgamesh sat at his side, his broad shoulders hunched and his hands gripping the edge of the wooden chair as though the strength of his hold could anchor his friend to the world of the living. Enkidu had grown weaker since the gods' decree had been made known, his once-vibrant presence dimmed as though the life was slipping from him in slow, deliberate increments. Gilgamesh, for all his strength, could do nothing but watch, helpless and furious.

The faint light of dawn crept into the chamber, casting a pale glow on Enkidu's face. He stirred slightly, his brow furrowing as his lips moved, forming words too faint for Gilgamesh to hear. Leaning closer, Gilgamesh placed a hand on Enkidu's shoulder.

"Enkidu," he said softly. "What do you see?"

Enkidu's eyes fluttered open, their usual sharpness dulled. He turned his head slightly, his gaze meeting Gilgamesh's with a mixture of weariness and sorrow. "I dreamed again," he said, his voice a faint rasp. "The gods speak to me in my dreams, and their voices are as cold and unforgiving as the winds of the steppe."

Gilgamesh's jaw tightened, his fists clenching as though he could fight the invisible forces conspiring against his friend. "Tell me," he urged. "What did you see?"

Enkidu closed his eyes, his expression pained as the memory of the dream flooded back to him. "I saw myself standing at the gates of a great, dark house," he said, his words halting. "A place of dust and shadow, where the air is thick with silence and despair. The house was vast, its walls stretching endlessly, and within it lived those who had gone before. They wore feathers like the wings of birds, and their faces were hollow, their eyes empty of light. They sat in the darkness, eating clay and drinking murky water, their lives reduced to the barest existence."

Gilgamesh's heart ached at the vividness of Enkidu's description. "And these beings," he asked, his voice strained. "Did they speak to you?"

Enkidu nodded weakly. "They spoke without words, their silence heavier than any sound. They seemed to mock me, their presence a reminder of the fate that awaits me. I saw myself among them, bound and captive, my strength gone, my name forgotten."

Gilgamesh shook his head, his voice filled with defiance. "That will not be your fate," he said firmly. "You are no ordinary man, Enkidu. Your name will not be lost in the dust. I will ensure it is remembered for all time."

Enkidu's lips twitched into a faint smile, though it was laced with sadness. "You have always been the dreamer, Gilgamesh," he said. "But even you cannot challenge the will of the gods."

Gilgamesh leaned forward, his voice fierce. "I can, and I will. If the gods believe they can take you from me, they will learn the strength of my defiance."

Enkidu reached out a trembling hand, his grip weak but his intent strong. "Do not let your grief consume you," he said. "There is no shame in accepting what cannot be changed. But before I go, there is something I must do."

Gilgamesh frowned, confused. "What is it?"

Enkidu closed his eyes, his voice trembling with emotion. "I have cursed those who led me to this life," he said. "The trapper who brought me out of the wilderness. Shamhat, who fed me and clothed me, who showed me the ways of men. In my anger, I cursed them, but I see now that I was wrong."

Gilgamesh listened intently, his heart heavy with the weight of Enkidu's regret.

"Shamhat," Enkidu continued, his voice softening. "She did not harm me. She opened my eyes to the world beyond the wild. Without her, I would never have known you, Gilgamesh. I would never have known friendship, love, and the joy of standing beside you in battle. I bless her for the life she gave me, for the moments of beauty and strength I have known."

Tears pricked Gilgamesh's eyes, his throat tightening as he listened to his friend's words. "She would be honored to hear that," he said quietly. "You have been a gift to us all, Enkidu. And I will make sure she knows the truth of your heart."

As the day wore on, Enkidu drifted in and out of consciousness, his strength ebbing like the tide. Gilgamesh remained by his side, unwilling to leave even for a moment. When Enkidu stirred again, his expression was strained, his features drawn tight with fear.

"I dreamed again," he whispered, his voice barely audible.

Gilgamesh leaned closer, his chest tightening with dread. "What did you see?"

Enkidu's eyes opened, filled with a haunting light. "I saw the Netherworld," he said, his voice trembling. "I was taken there, bound by chains I could not break. The ground beneath me was dust, the air thick and suffocating. I saw the gates of the great house swing open, and I was pulled inside."

He paused, his breath catching as tears slipped down his cheeks. "It was a place of darkness, Gilgamesh. A house with no light, no warmth. The walls were lined with shadows, and the air was filled with whispers that spoke of despair. The dead were there, their faces empty and lifeless, their eyes devoid of hope. They sat in silence, eating clay, their hands trembling as they reached for nothing."

Gilgamesh's heart broke as he listened, his fists clenching in helpless anger. "And what did they say to you?" he asked, his voice thick with emotion.

"They said nothing," Enkidu replied, his voice barely above a whisper. "Their silence was worse than any words. I was among them, Gilgamesh, stripped of my strength, my voice, my name. I was nothing."

Gilgamesh shook his head, his voice filled with fierce determination. "You are not nothing," he said, his voice trembling. "You are Enkidu, my dearest of friends, my equal. Your name will not fade into the shadows. It will be spoken for generations, a beacon of strength and loyalty."

Enkidu's eyes softened, his expression one of deep gratitude. "You are the greatest king, Gilgamesh," he said. "But you are also the greatest friend. Do not let my fate diminish you. Let it drive you to achieve the immortality we once sought together."

Gilgamesh nodded, his throat tight as he struggled to find words. "I will honor you, Enkidu," he said at last. "And I will ensure that the world remembers the man who stood beside me, for I love him."

Chapter 18:

THE DEATH OF A HERO

The days following the gods' decree were cloaked in a grief that seemed to seep into the very stones of Uruk. Though the sun shone and life in the city continued, the world felt dimmer, as if some invisible shadow had passed over the land. Gilgamesh, once the unshakable king, carried the weight of helplessness on his broad shoulders. His defiance had always been his greatest strength, but now it seemed to crumble under the inevitability of Enkidu's fate.

At first, the changes in Enkidu were subtle, almost unnoticeable. He regained some life that was still fleeting, yet he was able to move. He moved slower, his steps heavy, his laughter more fleeting. He dismissed it as fatigue, brushing away Gilgamesh's concern with a gruff smile. "I'm no weaker than I was when we fought Humbaba," he said, his voice firm but lacking its usual vigor. "It will pass. I may be getting stronger."

But it did not pass. Each day chipped away at Enkidu's strength once again. His powerful frame, once the very embodiment of life and vitality, began to wither. The sharpness in his eyes dulled, and the wild energy that had defined him seemed to drain away like water slipping through his fingers. Gilgamesh, consumed with plans to appeal to the gods or challenge their will, refused to acknowledge what was happening.

"You are stronger than this," he said one morning, his voice trembling despite his attempt to sound resolute. "This is not how it ends. I won't let it."

Enkidu, reclining against a pile of cushions in the palace chamber, managed a weak smile. "Even you, Gilgamesh, cannot hold back the tide. I was created by the gods, and now they call me back to them."

Gilgamesh refused to hear it. He summoned healers from across Uruk and beyond, offering them treasures and promises of favor if they could restore Enkidu. Priests filled the palace halls with incense and chants, calling upon the gods for mercy. Rituals were performed day and night, the air thick with the scent of burnt offerings. Yet, despite their efforts, Enkidu's condition worsened.

On the fourth day, he could no longer rise from his bed. By the seventh, his voice had grown faint, his words a struggle. Gilgamesh stayed at his side constantly, gripping his hand as though his strength alone could keep him tethered to life. He spoke to Enkidu of their adventures, trying to ignite a spark of the fire that had once burned so brightly within him.

"Do you remember," Gilgamesh asked one night, his voice thick with emotion, "how we faced Humbaba together? How the forest trembled as we struck him down? You said we were unstoppable. Two halves of the same whole."

Enkidu opened his eyes, the faintest glimmer of life flickering in them. "I remember," he whispered. "And I would do it all again. For you."

The nights were the hardest for Gilgamesh. He sat vigil by Enkidu's bed, his heart aching with every labored breath his friend took. Sleep eluded him, his mind a whirlwind of memories and unanswered questions. Why had the gods condemned them? Why had they given Enkidu life only to take it away? For the first time in his life, Gilgamesh felt powerless.

On the tenth night, Enkidu stirred, his voice faint but clear.

"Gilgamesh," he said, his gaze unfocused. "I dreamed again."

Gilgamesh leaned closer, his chest tightening with fear. "Tell me," he urged. "What did you see?" He knew by now that it would be a repeat of the previous dreams. His death was near.

"I was taken to a great house," Enkidu said, his voice trembling. "A place of shadows and dust, where the air is thick and heavy. The walls stretched endlessly, and within them were the dead. They sat in silence, their eyes empty, their hands grasping at nothing. They ate clay and drank from stagnant pools. I was among them, a prisoner in a house with no doors."

Gilgamesh's breath caught, his hands trembling as he gripped Enkidu's. "That will not be your fate," he said fiercely. "You are not nothing. You are Enkidu."

Enkidu's lips twitched into a faint smile. "The gods may take my life, but they cannot take what we have shared. You must carry on, Gilgamesh. Do not let grief consume you. Promise me."

"I promise," Gilgamesh whispered, tears slipping down his cheeks as he repeated what he had spoken before. "I will honor you in all that I do."

As the twelfth day dawned, Enkidu lay still, his breathing shallow, his body frail. The first rays of light filtered through the chamber, illuminating his face. Gilgamesh sat beside him, his hand clasping Enkidu's, his heart pounding as though trying to make up for the slowing beats of his friend's.

Enkidu's eyes fluttered open one last time, his gaze soft but steady. "Live, Gilgamesh," he said, his voice barely audible. "Live for both of us."

With that, his hand went limp, and his eyes closed. The breath left his body, and the wild man who had been Gilgamesh's equal, his companion, was gone.

Gilgamesh cried out, his voice raw and filled with anguish.

He clung to Enkidu's lifeless body, refusing to let go, his mind unable to comprehend what had happened. He whispered his friend's name, over and over, as though the sound of it could bring him back. Days passed, and still Gilgamesh would not leave Enkidu's side. He spoke to him as if he could still hear, recounting their adventures, their dreams, their plans.

But then, on the third day, the first signs of decay began to set in. A maggot emerged from Enkidu's nose, its small, insignificant form a devastating symbol of mortality. Gilgamesh froze, the sight shattering the last vestiges of denial he had clung to. His brother was truly gone.

The cry that tore from his throat echoed through the palace, a sound of unfiltered grief that silenced all who heard it. The people of Uruk, hearing their king's sorrow, wept openly. They mourned not just the loss of a hero, but the breaking of a bond that had inspired them all.

Chapter 19:

GRIEF'S DEPTHS

The palace of Uruk, once a place of grandeur and vitality, now lay cloaked in a profound and unrelenting silence. Gilgamesh, the great king whose voice once commanded the respect of his people and the fear of his enemies, now sat in the shadow of his grief. His throne, adorned with lapis lazuli and gold, felt hollow beneath him. Before him, the body of Enkidu rested, lifeless but still radiant with the memory of his strength and courage.

For days, Gilgamesh had stayed by his side, refusing food, sleep, or even the counsel of his advisors. He had spoken to Enkidu as though he were still alive, willing his brother to answer. But now, even his formidable will could not deny the truth. Enkidu was gone, claimed by the gods in a cruel act of retribution that Gilgamesh could neither understand nor forgive.

The dawn that followed Enkidu's passing broke with a quiet, golden light, but to Gilgamesh, it was as if the sun had lost its warmth. He rose from his vigil, his movements heavy with exhaustion and despair. Standing before the still form of his friend, he let out a cry of anguish that echoed through the palace halls, shaking the hearts of all who heard it.

"Mountains of cedar," Gilgamesh began, his voice breaking as he addressed the unseen forces of the world, "you who stood witness to our triumphs, now bow your heads and mourn for my beloved. Forests, whose shade gave us comfort, let your trees weep with the weight of my sorrow. Fields, rivers, and streams, you who watched our journey, flow with the tears that I cannot shed alone. Wild animals, companions of Enkidu's early life, howl your grief to the heavens, for the one who walked among you has been taken."

He turned to the people of Uruk, who had gathered in silent reverence, their faces pale with shared sorrow. "People of my city, raise your voices in mourning," he said, his tone commanding but filled with pain. "Cry out for Enkidu, who was more than a man. He was my brother, my equal, my heart. Mourn for the one who gave his strength to protect you, who stood beside me against the wrath of the gods."

The crowd began to weep openly, their grief flowing like a tide as they joined their king in his lament. Gilgamesh tore at his hair, the dark strands falling in tufts to the ground, and ripped his fine robes until they hung in tatters. His anguish was raw, unrestrained, a reflection of the bond that had been severed too soon. He recounted their adventures, his voice trembling as he spoke of the Cedar Forest and the battle against Humbaba, the journey that had solidified their friendship and revealed the strength they shared.

"Do you remember, Enkidu?" he whispered, his voice thick with tears. "Do you remember how we laughed at the edge of the forest, our hearts fearless even in the face of death? Do you remember the Bull of Heaven, how we stood together and defied the gods themselves? You gave me courage, Enkidu. You gave me purpose. Without you, I am a shadow."

Determined to honor Enkidu in death as he had in life, Gilgamesh commanded that a great funerary statue be commissioned. He summoned the finest artisans in Uruk, their talents renowned across the lands, and set them to work crafting a likeness of Enkidu that would capture his strength and spirit. They worked tirelessly, their hands guided by the memory of the man they sought to immortalize. The statue, carved from the finest stone and adorned with gold and precious jewels, stood tall and proud, a tribute to the greatness of the one it represented.

Gilgamesh did not stop there. From his treasury, he brought forth treasures of unimaginable value. There were golden vessels, jeweled ornaments, and silken robes, all to be offered to the gods of the Netherworld. He spared no expense, determined to ensure that Enkidu would be received favorably in the realm of the dead. These gifts, he hoped, would speak of the love and honor he bore.

As the preparations for Enkidu's burial were completed, Gilgamesh declared that a great banquet would be held in his honor. The palace was filled with the aroma of roasted meats and spiced wine, the finest delicacies laid out for the gods as offerings. Priests chanted solemn prayers, their voices rising and falling like waves, calling upon the deities of the Netherworld to accept Enkidu with grace. The banquet was not one of celebration but of reverence, a final act of devotion to the man who had touched so many lives.

When the time came for Enkidu's burial, Gilgamesh made a decision that reflected the depth of his grief and the magnitude of his love. The great river that ran through land, a lifeline of the city, was dammed temporarily to create a bed for Enkidu's tomb. The waters, diverted by the labor of hundreds, revealed a dry expanse where the tomb was to be placed. Within this sacred space, Enkidu's body was laid to rest, surrounded by treasures and offerings that glimmered in the dim light.

As the river waters were released, they surged back to their course, enveloping the tomb and creating a final, eternal resting place for Enkidu. The river itself became a symbol of his spirit, its waters flowing endlessly, carrying his memory through the lands. Gilgamesh stood at the edge of the waters, his eyes fixed on the place where his friend now rested. His heart, though heavy, was filled with a sense of purpose.

"Your name will not be forgotten," he said softly, the words carried away by the breeze. "I will ensure that your deeds, your courage, and your love are remembered for all time. This I swear, Enkidu."

As the sun set, casting the city in hues of gold and crimson, Gilgamesh turned from the river, his face etched with grief but also with resolve. Enkidu's death was not the end of their story—it was the beginning of a journey that would shape the fate of a king, a kingdom, and a legend.

Chapter 20:

WHY MUST WE DIE?

The streets, once alive with bustling energy, had grown subdued, as though the city itself mourned the loss of Enkidu. Merchants still plied their wares, and artisans still worked their craft, but an invisible weight hung over the people. It was a grief that seemed to seep into the very stones of the city, casting a shadow that lingered in every corner. The laughter of children, the chatter of markets, even the temple chants felt muted, as though the city dared not disturb the sorrow of its king.

Gilgamesh, for his part, wandered the streets aimlessly, a figure both familiar and foreign to his people. His once-commanding presence, so often a source of awe and pride, now seemed diminished. He wore the skins of animals, their coarse texture clinging to his body like a second grief. His hair was unkempt, and his eyes, once sharp with determination, were dull with loss. He avoided the palace and its trappings of power, finding no comfort in its grandeur. The places where he and Enkidu had once shared moments of joy, places like the courtyards filled with laughter, sparring grounds where their strength had been tested. These were now silent, haunted by the echo of memories.

At night, Gilgamesh sat alone in the vast emptiness of the palace's great hall, staring into the flickering flames of the hearth. The firelight danced across his features, casting shadows that seemed to mock him, taking the shape of his lost friend. He saw Enkidu in the flames, in the stillness of the night, in every quiet moment. He heard his laughter in the wind and felt his absence in every breath. The king who had faced gods and monsters with unflinching courage now found himself consumed by despair.

Grief was not the only weight on Gilgamesh's heart. Enkidu's death had forced him to confront a fear he had long buried. That of his own mortality. For all his strength and glory, he was still a man, bound to the same fate as his friend. The thought terrified him. What was the point of his achievements, his conquests, if they would all crumble into dust? What was the purpose of greatness if death awaited him at the end of his journey?

One night, unable to bear the suffocating stillness of the palace, Gilgamesh left and wandered the darkened streets of Uruk. The city was quiet, its inhabitants long since retired to their homes. The towering ziggurat of the temple loomed above him, its shadow stretching across the empty marketplace. He walked without direction, his thoughts a tumult of grief and anger.

"What is the purpose of it all?" he muttered to himself, his voice low and raw with anguish. "What is the point of building walls, of achieving greatness, if it all crumbles into nothing? If even the greatest among us are destined to die?"

He stopped at the edge of the city, where the walls of Uruk met the vast plains beyond. The wilderness stretched out before him, a reminder of Enkidu's origins. The open expanse called to him, its silence both comforting and ominous. He looked up at the sky, his gaze searching the stars for some sign, some answer. But the heavens remained silent, indifferent to his pain.

As dawn broke over the horizon, painting the sky with hues of gold and crimson, Gilgamesh made a decision. The wilderness, which had once seemed so alien to him, now felt like the only place where he might find clarity. He could no longer sit idly in the city, surrounded by memories of what he had lost. He needed answers about life, death, and the gods' decree.

"I will not accept this," he said, his voice steady despite the tremor of emotion. "I will not allow death to be the end. There must be a way to defy it, to transcend it. I will find it, no matter the cost."

This decision gave him purpose, a direction to channel his grief. But it also gave rise to questions that burned within him. What lay beyond death? Was there truly an underworld where Enkidu's soul resided? And if so, could he reach him? These questions gnawed at his mind, driving him to seek answers that no mortal had ever dared to pursue.

Gilgamesh sought out the priests and scholars of Uruk, demanding knowledge of the afterlife and the nature of mortality. He listened as they described the underworld, a shadowy realm where the dead wandered in eternal despair, stripped of their earthly identities. Their words offered no solace, only a grim confirmation of his fears.

"The gods have decreed the fate of mortals, my king," one priest said, his voice heavy with resignation. "None can escape it, not even you."

But Gilgamesh refused to accept this. He immersed himself in the temple archives, poring over ancient texts in search of hope. It was there that he learned of Utnapishtim, the man who had been granted immortality by the gods after surviving the great flood. If one man had escaped death, then perhaps there was a way for others. The idea took root in Gilgamesh's mind, growing into an obsession.

Driven by this newfound purpose, Gilgamesh began preparing for a journey unlike any he had undertaken before. He would seek out Utnapishtim, no matter the distance, no matter the dangers. If there was a secret to immortality, he would find it. If he could not escape death himself, then perhaps he could ensure that Enkidu's memory would endure forever.

As he prepared to leave, the sun god Shamash appeared to him in a blaze of golden light. Shamash, who had guided him and Enkidu through so many trials, now regarded him with a mixture of sorrow and concern.

"Gilgamesh," Shamash said, his voice filled with divine authority, "you are a king, a shepherd to your people. Your strength and wisdom are meant for the living. Why do you now abandon your city to seek what the gods have decreed no mortal can possess?"

Gilgamesh stood firm, his grief and determination etched into his features. "I cannot sit idly while death waits for me," he said. "I cannot accept a fate where all I have built, all I have loved, turns to dust. I must know if there is more. Is there a way to defy the silence of the grave?"

Shamash sighed, his light dimming slightly. "You chase a dream that has eluded even the greatest of mortals. But I see the fire in your heart, and I know you will not be swayed. Go, Gilgamesh. Seek the answers you crave, but know this, that the journey will cost you more than you can imagine."

With Shamash's warning echoing in his ears, Gilgamesh left Uruk, clad in the rough skins of animals and armed only with his grief and determination. The wilderness stretched before him, vast and unyielding, but he walked forward without hesitation. He was a king, a warrior, and a brother searching for answers in a world that seemed bent on denying them. And so, the greatest journey of his life began, driven by love, loss, and the unrelenting question that burned within him. Why must mortals die?

Chapter 21:

A QUEST BEGINS

The city faded behind Gilgamesh, its once-imposing walls diminishing into the vastness of the horizon. The once cries of merchants, the rhythmic pounding of the smiths' hammers, and the laughter of children became distant echoes, swallowed by the wilderness. The life he had known, the kingdom he had built, now felt like a fleeting mirage as he ventured deeper into the unknown. The rising sun cast long shadows across the rolling plains, painting the land in hues of gold and crimson, a stark contrast to the weight of grief that pressed upon his heart.

Enkidu's death was an unhealed wound, a raw and constant ache that gnawed at Gilgamesh's thoughts. The memories of their shared triumphs, laughter, and unbreakable bond were both a comfort and a torment. Death had taken Enkidu, and with him, it had stolen Gilgamesh's sense of invincibility. For the first time, the king who had bested gods and monsters felt small, mortal. Yet beneath the weight of his sorrow burned a fierce determination. If there was a way to defy death, to escape the fate that had claimed Enkidu, he would find it.

The tales of Utnapishtim consumed his mind. Known as "the Faraway," Utnapishtim was said to have survived the great flood, a deluge sent by the gods to cleanse the earth. In gratitude for his piety and the sacrifices he offered, the gods had granted him and his wife immortality. The thought of a mortal man who had cheated death, who lived eternally beyond the reach of time, ignited a desperate hope in Gilgamesh. If Utnapishtim had found a way, then so could he.

Gilgamesh traveled light. His blade, sharp and battle-tested, hung at his side. A flask of water and a pouch of dried provisions were his only other belongings. But the true weight he carried was not physical. It was the crushing sorrow of loss and the unrelenting question that haunted him. What is the purpose of life, if it ends in death?

At first, the plains surrounding Uruk were familiar. Golden grasses swayed in the wind, and the soft hum of the Tigris and Euphrates carried on the breeze. The occasional shade of a lone tree offered respite from the sun's relentless heat. These lands, so close to home, brought fleeting memories of Enkidu. Gilgamesh could almost hear his friend's voice, teasing him for his restlessness.

But as the days stretched into weeks, the landscape grew harsher. The sun became a merciless overseer, its heat baking the earth and searing Gilgamesh's skin. At night, the wilderness turned bitterly cold, the stars glinting like distant, unfeeling eyes. The silence pressed in around him, broken only by the occasional howl of a distant predator or the rustle of unseen creatures in the brush.

Through this inhospitable expanse, Gilgamesh pressed on, his grief and determination his only companions. Along the way, he encountered travelers. There were many, from caravans laden with spices and silks, shepherds guiding their flocks, and wandering minstrels singing songs of love and loss. They recognized their king instantly, their eyes wide with reverence and curiosity. Some fell to their knees, offering blessings and prayers, while others extended their hospitality by offering food, water, a place by the fire.

But Gilgamesh declined all but the most necessary sustenance. His journey was not one of comfort or distraction. He had no time for idle tales or fleeting companionship. He asked only one question of those he met. "Have you heard of Utnapishtim?"

Most responded with blank stares or the shake of a head. Others dismissed the question as folly. "A tale for children," one man said, laughing nervously. "No one cheats death, not even kings."

Yet, in the voices of a few, Gilgamesh found the faint threads of hope he sought.

"I have heard the name," an elderly merchant murmured one evening, his face half-lit by the flickering light of a campfire. "They say he lives at the edge of the world, beyond the mountains where the sun sets. But no mortal can reach him."

Another spoke of a treacherous path guarded by creatures of divine origin, of a land where no man could tread and return. Gilgamesh listened intently, committing every word to memory, the impossibility of the task only stoking the fire in his heart.

"No mortal can reach him," one wanderer said, his voice tinged with both awe and fear. "But you, my king… perhaps you are different."

Gilgamesh's jaw tightened at the words. He was different. He was two-thirds divine, born of Ninsun the goddess and Lugalbanda the king. If any man could reach Utnapishtim, it was him. "I am no ordinary mortal," he replied, his voice steady with conviction. "If Utnapishtim lives, I will find him. If he holds the secret to eternal life, I will take it."

His journey took him through deserts where the sands seemed to stretch endlessly, their golden waves shifting under the relentless sun. He crossed rivers swollen with spring rains, their currents threatening to pull him under, but he forged ahead. The wilderness tested him at every turn, but Gilgamesh met its challenges with the same resolve that had seen him face Humbaba and the Bull of Heaven. He was a man consumed, driven not only by the desire to escape death but by the memory of Enkidu.

Each night, as he set up a meager camp beneath the stars, Gilgamesh's thoughts turned inward. The grief that had first spurred him on now mixed with questions that gnawed at his soul. Was Utnapishtim truly immortal, or was he merely another myth, a story spun by desperate men to stave off their fear of death? If he found him, would he hold the answers Gilgamesh sought? And if immortality could be achieved, what would it mean to live forever in a world where even the brightest bonds could be severed?

As he neared the mountains spoken of in the legends, the terrain grew treacherous. The paths were steep and jagged, the air thin and cold. Yet Gilgamesh climbed with a purpose that defied exhaustion. His muscles burned, his lungs ached, but his resolve did not waver. Every step brought him closer to the answers he sought, to the hope that had kept him moving when despair threatened to consume him.

One evening, as the sun dipped below the horizon and painted the sky in fiery hues, Gilgamesh paused to rest on a rocky outcrop. The plains stretched out below him, vast and endless, a reminder of how far he had come. Yet the journey ahead loomed even larger.

Staring into the fading light, Gilgamesh spoke aloud, his voice carrying on the wind. "Enkidu," he said softly, the name a prayer and a lament. "I will not let your death be in vain. I will find the answers you sought, the answers we both need. I will defeat the gods themselves if I must."

As the stars began to emerge, their cold light glinting like the eyes of distant watchers, Gilgamesh closed his eyes. His heart burned with grief, with anger, with purpose. The journey to Utnapishtim was far from over, but he knew one thing with certainty, he would not stop. Not until he found the man who had cheated death, the man who held the secret that might bring meaning to the fragile, fleeting lives of mortals.

Chapter 22:

PRIDE AND GRIEF

The wilderness was vast and unrelenting, its expanse stretching endlessly under a sky that had turned a deep indigo. The mountain pass that Gilgamesh now traversed was harsh and unforgiving, its jagged peaks silhouetted against the faint glow of the stars. The air grew colder with every step, biting through the animal skins he wore and seeping into his bones. A sharp wind howled through the crags, carrying with it the eerie whispers of the wild. Yet Gilgamesh pressed on, his grief and determination shielding him from the discomforts of the journey.

The terrain was treacherous, littered with loose stones that threatened to give way underfoot. The moon hung low in the sky, its pale light offering only the faintest guidance. Each step was a calculated effort, his muscles burning with the strain of the climb. But Gilgamesh welcomed the challenge. The physical toil distracted him from the relentless ache in his heart, that same ache of Enkidu's absence and the oppressive weight of his own mortality.

The higher he climbed, the more the world seemed to shrink behind him. The plains and forests he had crossed were now distant shadows, obscured by the darkness. Uruk, his once-great city, felt like a memory from another life. Here, in the desolation of the mountains, he was not a king or a hero. He was simply a man, stripped of the trappings of power and glory, seeking answers in a world that seemed determined to keep them hidden.

The sound of distant growls reached his ears, low and guttural, carried on the wind. Gilgamesh halted, his hand instinctively moving to the hilt of his sword. His sharp eyes scanned the darkness, but the moonlight revealed nothing but the jagged outlines of rocks and the shifting shadows they cast. He stood motionless, his breath misting in the frigid air, his senses heightened.

The growls grew louder, more distinct, and were soon joined by the soft padding of paws against stone. A pride of lions emerged from the shadows, their golden eyes gleaming like molten fire in the dim light. Their movements were fluid and deliberate, their bodies rippling with muscle as they circled him, their growls low and menacing. The leader of the pride, a massive male with a dark mane that seemed to absorb the moonlight, stood at the forefront, his gaze locked onto Gilgamesh.

For a moment, Gilgamesh felt a flicker of fear. The lions were creatures of the wild, untamed and powerful, a force of nature that mirrored the raw energy Enkidu had once embodied. But the fear passed as quickly as it came, replaced by a steely resolve. He was Gilgamesh, the king who had slain Humbaba, who had defied the Bull of Heaven. He would not be cowed by beasts, no matter how fearsome.

Still, he knew better than to act without care. Slowly, he stepped back, retreating to a narrow alcove in the rock that offered some semblance of protection. The lions prowled closer, their growls deepening as they tested the boundaries of his space. He could see the glint of their teeth, the powerful sway of their bodies, and he knew that to face them directly in that moment would be folly.

As the wind whipped around him, Gilgamesh dropped to one knee and closed his eyes. He clasped his hands together, his voice low and steady as he addressed the moon god Sin, the celestial guardian of the night.

"Sin, lord of the silver light, hear my prayer," he said, his words carried by the wind. "You who watch over travelers in the darkness, guide me now. Protect me from the dangers that stalk this night and grant me the strength to overcome them. I seek not for glory, but for answers. I seek to defy the silence of the grave and honor the memory of Enkidu. Be my shield, and I shall face whatever comes."

The moonlight seemed to brighten slightly, casting a pale glow over the mountain pass. The growls of the lions softened, and though they still prowled around him, they did not attack. Gilgamesh took this as a sign, a moment of reprieve granted by the god he had invoked. He leaned back against the rock, his hand resting on the hilt of his sword, and allowed his weary body to succumb to sleep.

His dreams were vivid and strange, filled with symbols and visions that seemed to speak to him in a language beyond words. He saw a great river, its waters shimmering with silver light, carrying him toward a distant shore. On the banks of the river stood Enkidu, his form strong and whole, his eyes filled with a calm that Gilgamesh had never seen in life. Enkidu raised a hand, gesturing for him to follow, and though the dream shifted before he could reach his friend, Gilgamesh awoke with a sense of clarity and resolve.

The lions were still there, their golden eyes watching him intently as he rose to his feet. They moved as a single entity, their bodies taut with potential energy, but Gilgamesh was no longer paralyzed by their presence. He unsheathed his sword, the blade catching the moonlight as he held it aloft.

"You have tested me," he said aloud, his voice steady and commanding. "Now I will show you the strength of a man who seeks immortality."

The leader of the pride lunged first, its massive form a blur of golden fur and muscle. Gilgamesh met the attack head-on, his sword slicing through the air with precision born of countless battles. The blade struck true, and the lion let out a deafening roar as it fell to the ground. The others followed, their movements coordinated and deadly, but Gilgamesh moved with a fury fueled by purpose and grief. He was unrelenting, his blade flashing in the moonlight as he fought with the desperation of a man who had nothing left to lose.

One by one, the lions fell, their roars echoing through the mountain pass until only silence remained. Gilgamesh stood amidst their fallen forms, his breath coming in ragged gasps, his body trembling with exertion. The blood of the beasts stained the ground around him, a stark reminder of the battle that had just unfolded.

He knelt by the largest lion, the leader of the pride, and ran his hand over its mane. "You were a worthy opponent," he said quietly, his voice tinged with respect. "But my journey is not yet over."

With the strength that remained, Gilgamesh skinned the lions, their hides heavy but warm. He fashioned them into cloaks, their golden fur a shield against the cold that had seeped into his bones. As he wrapped himself in their warmth, he felt a flicker of something he had not felt since Enkidu's death. He felt hope.

Chapter 23:

THE SCORPION GATEKEEPERS

The twin peaks of Mount Mashu loomed before Gilgamesh, their jagged spires reaching into the heavens like the claws of some primordial beast. These mountains were myth incarnate, the boundary between the known world and the divine mysteries that lay beyond. It was said that here, at the very edge of the earth, the sun god Shamash entered the underworld each night to begin his journey beneath the earth, emerging only at dawn. To Gilgamesh, they were a threshold. They were a gate he must pass to reach Utnapishtim, the Faraway, and the secret of eternal life.

The journey to this place had drained him. The mountains rose abruptly from the wilderness, their cliffs black and foreboding, their peaks cloaked in wisps of cold mist. The path leading to their base was strewn with boulders and lined with strange, twisted trees that seemed to whisper in the biting wind. The air itself felt different here, charged with an almost oppressive presence, as though the mountains were aware of his approach.

At the base of the peaks stood the gates of Mashu, enormous slabs of obsidian that shimmered faintly even in the dim light. They were etched with intricate carvings that seemed to shift when he looked too long, patterns forming and dissolving like smoke caught in a breeze. The gates were shut, their surface emanating a faint hum that vibrated in his bones. He stepped forward, his resolve unwavering despite the chill that raced down his spine.

Two figures emerged from the shadows flanking the gates. They were unlike anything Gilgamesh had ever seen, their forms a fusion of human and monstrous. The upper halves of their bodies were those of tall, imposing warriors, clad in gleaming armor that seemed to flow like liquid metal. Their lower halves, however, were grotesque, segmented and chitinous like the bodies of scorpions, their massive tails arching high above them, stingers glinting with a venomous sheen. Their eyes glowed faintly, unblinking and filled with a knowledge that felt ancient and unfathomable.

The larger of the two stepped forward, its deep voice reverberating like the rumble of distant thunder. "Who dares approach the gates of Mashu?" it demanded, its luminous gaze fixing on Gilgamesh. "Who seeks to pass where no mortal has tread without falling into darkness?"

Gilgamesh, weary but resolute, squared his shoulders. "I am Gilgamesh, king of Uruk," he said, his voice steady despite the enormity of the beings before him. "I seek Utnapishtim, the one who holds the secret of eternal life. My journey is one of purpose, born of grief and defiance. I will not turn back."

The smaller gatekeeper tilted its head, its tail twitching ominously. "You seek what is forbidden," it said, its voice higher but no less chilling. "The path you desire leads to death or madness. Turn back now, mortal, before the gods claim you as they have claimed all who came before."

Gilgamesh's grief flared into anger, his fists clenching. "I have lost my brother, Enkidu, to the decree of the gods. I refuse to accept their judgment. I will find the answers I seek, even if it means defying death itself. If you are the guardians of this place, then test me, for I will not leave without passage."

The larger gatekeeper studied him in silence for a moment, its glowing eyes inscrutable. Finally, it spoke. "You carry the weight of sorrow and the fire of purpose. Yet the path beyond these gates is not for the faint of heart. To proceed, you must prove yourself. You must prove your strength, your resolve, and your understanding of the truths that bind all things."

The smaller gatekeeper gestured toward a massive stone slab embedded in the ground before the gates. Its surface was inscribed with glowing runes, their light shifting and flickering like fireflies caught in amber. "These are the riddles of the gods," it said. "Answer them truthfully, or perish where you stand."

Gilgamesh stepped forward, his heart pounding. He had faced many trials before, but this felt different. It felt less a test of his body and more a test of his very soul. He read the first riddle as it flared to life, the words etching themselves into his mind.

"What is stronger than the gods, more powerful than death, and yet humbler than the softest whisper?"

He frowned, his mind racing. The question was a paradox, a truth hidden in contradiction. He thought of Enkidu, of the bond they had shared, of the love that had driven him to this place. Slowly, he spoke. "It is the will of mortals," he said. "Though fleeting, our resolve and our love endure beyond the grasp of the gods."

The runes pulsed brightly before fading. The larger gatekeeper nodded. "You have answered true. But there are two more."

The second riddle ignited on the stone, its glow sharper than before.

"What walks beside every man, yet is unseen? What cannot be outrun, yet is forever behind him?"

The answer came to Gilgamesh immediately, its truth cutting through him like a blade. He thought of the shadow that had followed him since Enkidu's death. "It is death," he said, his voice quieter. "It is always with us, and though we may flee, it remains."

The runes vanished again, and the gatekeepers exchanged a

glance. The smaller one's stinger arched higher, its voice carrying an edge of tension. "You see clearly, mortal. But clarity alone will not suffice. The final question awaits."

The last riddle glowed golden, its words steady and deliberate.

"What remains when all else is gone? What binds the living and the dead, the gods and the earth, in an unbreakable chain?"

Gilgamesh hesitated, the weight of the question pressing on him. He thought of the emptiness left by Enkidu's death, the bond that still connected them despite the grave. The answer came not as a revelation but as a truth he had always known. "It is love," he said, his voice steady. "Love endures beyond death, beyond the gods themselves. It is the force that gives life meaning."

The runes flared brilliantly before disappearing entirely. The gatekeepers stepped aside, their expressions grave. "You have answered true," the larger one said. "Your understanding of these truths has granted you passage. But know this, the path ahead will demand more than strength or wisdom. It will demand your very soul."

The gates groaned as they began to open, revealing a dark tunnel that stretched into the heart of the mountains. The air beyond was cool and heavy, carrying the faint sound of rushing water and whispers that seemed to come from nowhere. Gilgamesh took a deep breath, steeling himself, and stepped forward.

As he passed through, the smaller gatekeeper called after him. "Beware the shadows, king of Uruk. In seeking to conquer death, you may lose what it means to truly live."

Gilgamesh did not look back. The weight of their words settled on him, but he carried them with his grief and his purpose as he entered the tunnel. The light of the gates faded behind him, and he descended into the unknown, every step taking him closer to Utnapishtim and the answers he sought.

Chapter 24:

THE PATH OF DARKNESS

The gates of Mashu sealed behind Gilgamesh with a deep, echoing groan, the sound reverberating through the cavernous space like the finality of a tomb. Darkness swallowed him whole, so absolute that it seemed to press against his skin. It was a void devoid of stars or light, where the boundaries of the world blurred into nothingness. The air was damp and cold, carrying the scent of ancient stone and the faint, metallic tang of the earth's core.

Gilgamesh paused, his breath steady but shallow, as the enormity of the Path of Darkness unfolded before him. This was the tunnel of the sun god Shamash, where the sun traveled in shadow to rise again each day. No mortal had dared tread this path and lived to tell of it, for it was a place where time and space twisted, where light was a memory and darkness a living thing. Yet Gilgamesh pressed forward. The memory of Enkidu, the weight of his grief, and the burning desire to defy death propelled him into the black abyss.

His first steps were cautious, his hands outstretched to feel the jagged stone walls on either side. The rough surface scraped his fingertips, grounding him in a world that felt increasingly unreal. The crunch of rocks under his feet on the uneven ground echoed faintly before being swallowed by the void. With each step, the darkness seemed to deepen, as though the tunnel itself was alive, watching, waiting.

As he moved, whispers began to creep in at the edges of his hearing. They were not words but feelings, fragments of emotion that stirred the shadows. Fear, regret, and sorrow pressed in on him, each step dragging memories to the surface. He saw Enkidu's face, his fierce grin replaced by the pallor of death. He heard his laughter dissolve into ragged breaths. The pain was sharp, cutting through his resolve like a blade.

"You cannot save him," the shadows seemed to murmur. "You cannot save yourself. Turn back."

Gilgamesh's jaw clenched, his fists tightening at his sides. "I will not yield," he muttered, his voice echoing into the void. "I am Gilgamesh. I will not be broken by shadows."

The whispers did not abate, but Gilgamesh pressed on, his steps becoming surer even as the ground grew treacherous. Sharp stones cut into his feet, and the walls seemed to close in around him, narrowing until he was forced to crawl on his hands and knees. The cold bit into his skin, and exhaustion gnawed at his strength, but he refused to stop. Every scrape of his palms against the stone, every labored breath, was a defiance of the darkness that sought to consume him.

Hours passed. Perhaps days. Time lost all meaning in the eternal black. Hunger clawed at his stomach, and thirst dried his throat, but Gilgamesh pressed forward. His resolve was his only light, his grief his only companion. The whispers became louder, mocking and insidious, feeding on his fatigue.

"Why do you struggle?" they hissed. "You are mortal. You will die as he did. All your strength, all your glory, will crumble into dust."

At one point, he stumbled, his foot catching on an unseen stone. He fell hard, the breath driven from his lungs as his knees struck the ground. His blade clattered away into the dark. For a moment, he lay still, the cold stone pressing against his cheek, his chest heaving with the effort of breathing. Despair loomed, a heavy weight that threatened to crush him.

But then, from the depths of his memory, Enkidu's voice rose unbidden. He heard his laughter, the fire in his words as they faced the Bull of Heaven. He saw the wild joy in his eyes as they stood side by side in the Cedar Forest. The bond they had shared burned brighter than the darkness around him.

"Get up," Gilgamesh whispered to himself, his voice raw but determined. "For him. For the promise you made."

With a groan, he pushed himself to his knees, then to his feet. His body screamed in protest, but his spirit blazed with renewed strength. He retrieved his blade and continued, each step an act of defiance.

Finally, after what felt like an eternity, the darkness began to shift. A faint glow appeared ahead, so dim at first that he thought it a trick of his mind. But as he moved closer, the light grew, illuminating the walls of the tunnel with a soft, golden hue. The air warmed, carrying a faint, floral scent that was almost intoxicating after the oppressive cold of the void.

Gilgamesh emerged into a vast cavern, its ceiling so high it disappeared into shadow. The walls sparkled with veins of crystal, refracting the golden light into a kaleidoscope of brilliance. At the center of the cavern lay a pool of water, its surface so still it mirrored the light perfectly. Around the pool grew flowers that glowed faintly, their petals delicate and luminous.

Kneeling at the water's edge, Gilgamesh cupped his hands and drank deeply. The cool liquid slid down his throat, invigorating him in a way no mortal drink ever had. It seemed to seep into his very being, restoring his strength and sharpening his senses. He sat back, his gaze drifting over the serene beauty of the cavern.

The silence here was different. It was peaceful, not oppressive. It felt as though the space itself was alive, a sanctuary carved from the bones of the earth. For the first time since entering the tunnel,

Gilgamesh allowed himself to breathe deeply, to let the calm wash over him. But he did not linger. This was not his destination.

Rising on unsteady legs, he turned his gaze to the far end of the cavern, where the tunnel continued into shadow. The faint glow of the cavern faded behind him as he stepped forward, the darkness returning but no longer absolute. His steps were surer now, his resolve strengthened by the trials he had endured.

He walked for what felt like another lifetime, the tunnel narrowing and twisting, but no longer did it feel hostile. The whispers of doubt and fear had receded, their power diminished by his unwavering will. At last, a brighter light appeared ahead, spilling into the tunnel like the promise of dawn. It was the eastern exit, the end of the Path of Darkness.

Gilgamesh quickened his pace, his heart pounding as he stepped into the light. The air here was warm, carrying the scent of earth and life. He emerged onto a plateau, the vast wilderness stretching out before him, bathed in the golden hues of a rising sun. He turned back to the tunnel, its mouth a dark maw behind him, and exhaled deeply.

The Path of Darkness had tested him, stripping away his illusions and forcing him to confront his deepest fears. But he had endured. He had not come this far to falter. Somewhere beyond the horizon, Utnapishtim awaited, and with him, the answers that Gilgamesh sought.

Standing beneath the vast expanse of the sky, he felt the warmth of the sun on his face and the memory of Enkidu at his side. For the first time in what felt like an eternity, Gilgamesh allowed himself a faint smile. His journey was far from over, but he had crossed a threshold that few would dare.

Chapter 25:

GARDEN OF THE GODS

When Gilgamesh emerged from the suffocating darkness of the Path of Shamash, he stumbled into a world so radiant and surreal that it seemed to belong to a dream. The oppressive weight of the tunnel fell away, replaced by a sense of openness and wonder so profound that it brought him to a standstill. He stood at the edge of the Garden of the Gods, and for a moment, he simply stared, awestruck.

The garden stretched endlessly before him, a paradise alive with light and life. The air was warm and fragrant, filled with the mingled scents of blooming flowers and ripe fruit. It was unlike anything he had known, a world untainted by death or decay. The light was neither harsh nor dim but a golden glow that seemed to emanate from the very air, suffusing everything it touched with a gentle radiance.

Trees of unimaginable beauty filled the landscape, their branches heavy with fruit that shimmered like jewels. Golden apples, emerald pears, and crimson pomegranates hung alongside strange, otherworldly fruits in hues that defied mortal understanding. Their glow painted the trees in a kaleidoscope of colors, their light refracted through leaves of silver and gold. The ground beneath his feet was soft and lush, a carpet of grass so vibrant that it seemed to hum with life.

Streams of crystalline water meandered lazily through the garden, their surfaces catching the light and scattering it in dazzling patterns. Birds of incredible colors flitted between the trees, their plumage reflecting every hue of the spectrum. Their songs were unlike anything Gilgamesh had heard, a melody that seemed to awaken forgotten parts of his soul, stirring emotions he could not name.

"This," he murmured, his voice barely above a whisper, "is a place untouched by death. A sanctuary where the gods must dwell."

He took a tentative step forward, his feet sinking slightly into the impossibly soft earth. Each step felt reverent, a journey deeper into a sacred realm. The pain of his grief, the weight of Enkidu's loss, seemed to soften in the presence of such overwhelming beauty. Yet it did not leave him entirely. It remained, a quiet ache that reminded him why he had come.

Gilgamesh wandered deeper into the garden, his eyes wide as he took in the wonders around him. He came upon a grove where the fruit trees stood in perfect symmetry, their branches laden with glowing treasures. Hunger gnawed at him, the grueling journey and his endless grief having left him physically drained. He reached for a golden apple, the fruit warm beneath his fingers and humming faintly with a life of its own.

As he held it, a voice slithered into his mind, soft and beguiling. "Eat, mortal," it whispered, the words curling around his thoughts like tendrils of smoke. "Taste of the fruit, and you shall know the secrets of this place. You shall become as the gods."

Startled, Gilgamesh turned to find a serpent coiled around the trunk of a nearby tree. Its emerald scales shimmered like polished gemstones, and its golden eyes gleamed with a knowing light. The serpent regarded him with a strange intelligence, its tongue flicking out as it spoke again.

"This is what you seek, is it not? Immortality. Power. To transcend the fate that claims all mortals. Eat, and it shall be yours."

For a moment, the temptation was overwhelming. The fruit seemed to pulse in his hand, its light promising all that he desired. Was this not the reason he had journeyed so far, endured so much? Yet as he gazed at the apple, another image rose unbidden in his mind. It was Enkidu's face, his fierce smile, and the bond they had shared. The memory cut through the serpent's words like a blade.

"No," Gilgamesh said, his voice firm. He hurled the apple to the ground, where it landed with a dull thud, its light dimming. "I will not take shortcuts. If I am to defy death, it will be through strength and resolve, not deception."

The serpent hissed, its golden eyes narrowing, but it said no more as Gilgamesh walked away.

Beyond the grove, he came to a clearing dominated by a magnificent fountain. It was carved from a single piece of translucent stone, its surface etched with flowing patterns that seemed to shift and dance in the light. Water cascaded from its peak in crystalline streams, pooling in a basin that glowed faintly. The sound of the water was soothing, its gentle rush a balm to his weary spirit.

Gilgamesh knelt by the fountain, his reflection rippling in the glowing pool. He did not see the face of a king or a warrior but that of a man worn by loss and longing. His grief was etched into the lines of his brow, his strength tempered by sorrow. He dipped his hands into the water, its coolness startling and invigorating. When he drank, it was as if the water carried with it a fragment of the garden's peace. For a moment, the weight of his journey lifted, and his thoughts grew clearer.

"This place is not for me," he murmured, rising to his feet. "Its peace is a trap. My journey does not end here."

Determined, he moved deeper into the garden. He crossed a meadow alive with colors, where flowers glowed like tiny stars and birds sang in harmonies that seemed to transcend mortal music. A stream of liquid silver wound its way through the grass, its surface gleaming like moonlight. He followed its course to a bridge carved from living stone, its intricate patterns depicting scenes of creation. The craftsmanship was so perfect that the figures seemed poised to move, their frozen gestures alive with potential.

Yet with every step, a faint unease began to stir in Gilgamesh's heart. The beauty of the garden was intoxicating, but it also felt too perfect, too complete. It was a place that seemed to whisper promises of solace, of rest, of forgetting. But Gilgamesh could not forget. He could not rest. This place, for all its wonders, was not his destination. It was a test, a challenge to his resolve, to his commitment to the memory of Enkidu and the purpose that had brought him here.

At last, he reached the edge of the garden, where a towering archway of living vines marked the boundary of this realm. Beyond the arch lay a path of golden sand, stretching into a horizon bathed in soft twilight. The air was cooler here, the garden's whispers fading into a contemplative silence. Gilgamesh paused, looking back one final time. The Garden of the Gods was everything the mortal world was not.. It felt eternal, unchanging, untouched by pain or death. It called to him, offering an escape from the trials that lay ahead.

But he turned away, stepping through the arch with unshakable resolve. The path before him was uncertain, its dangers and trials hidden in the twilight haze. Yet Gilgamesh walked forward, carrying with him the love he bore for Enkidu, the promise he had made, and the knowledge that his journey was far from over.

The garden faded behind him, its beauty a memory that would linger but not bind him. Gilgamesh pressed onward, his steps firm, his heart resolute, ready to face whatever lay ahead in his relentless pursuit of the answers that would defy the very gods and conquer death itself.

Chapter 26:

THE WATERS OF DEATH

The light from the Garden of the Gods had long faded behind Gilgamesh as he approached the edge of the world, his steps heavy with exhaustion yet propelled by a singular, unrelenting purpose. The path before him sloped downward, leading to a small, weathered structure perched precariously near the vast expanse of the Waters of Death. The house, built of sun-bleached wood and patched with bits of cloth and rope, seemed almost out of place, a fragile defiance against the desolation surrounding it. Smoke curled lazily from its crooked chimney, the only sign of life in this barren place.

Gilgamesh stopped a short distance from the house, his breath catching in his throat as he surveyed his surroundings. The sky above was a deep indigo, studded with cold, distant stars. The Waters of Death stretched out beyond the house, dark and foreboding, their surface unnaturally still. A faint, acrid wind drifted from the shoreline, carrying the scent of decay and ancient secrets. He swallowed hard, his heart pounding as he approached the door, his mind racing with the weight of his quest.

Inside, the small home was dimly lit by the fire crackling in a hearth at the far end of the room. The warmth was a sharp contrast to the chill outside, the flickering light casting long shadows across the walls. The space was simple but strangely inviting. Rough wooden furniture lay spread about with a few shelves on the wall lined with clay jars. There were faded tapestries that hinted at stories long forgotten. A single figure moved within, her back turned to him as she tended to a pot hanging over the fire.

She turned at the sound of him crossing the threshold, her expression sharp with suspicion. The woman was striking, her tall frame clad in a simple, flowing garment of earth-toned fabric. Her dark hair was braided with thin threads of gold, and her eyes that were piercing and perceptive seemed to take in every detail of Gilgamesh in an instant. This was Siduri, the alewife of legend, and her gaze lingered on him with a mixture of curiosity and caution.

"You," she said, her voice rich and melodic but edged with wariness. "Who are you, and why do you darken my door? You look as though the wilderness has devoured all but your shadow. Are you a murderer, a thief?"

Gilgamesh straightened, his hand instinctively brushing the hilt of his sword. "I am Gilgamesh, king of Uruk," he replied, his voice steady but raw with exhaustion. "I come not as a thief nor a murderer, but as a man seeking answers."

Siduri raised an eyebrow, her expression skeptical as she stepped closer, studying him. His disheveled appearance, from the dirt streaking his face to his torn and bloodied clothes spoke of hardship and desperation. "King of Uruk?" she echoed, a faint smile tugging at her lips. "You look more like a beggar than a king."

Gilgamesh met her gaze, unflinching. "Perhaps I am," he said. "I have cast aside my crown, my city, and my comforts to find Utnapishtim. I seek the secret of immortality."

Siduri's smile faded, replaced by a look of quiet understanding. She gestured for him to sit at the rough-hewn table in the center of the room, pouring a golden liquid into a clay cup and setting it before him. "Drink," she said. "You've come far, and your story deserves to be heard."

Gilgamesh hesitated, then took the cup. The liquid was warm and sweet, its richness spreading through his body and dulling the edges of his weariness. He set the cup down and looked at her, his eyes burning with determination. "Will you help me?"

Siduri sat across from him, folding her hands on the table. Her expression was unreadable, her gaze steady. "Tell me, Gilgamesh," she said softly. "What is it you hope to gain? Do you believe immortality will bring you peace? Will it bring back the one you have lost?"

"Enkidu," he said, his voice breaking as the name left his lips. "Death took him, and I could do nothing. I cannot accept that this is all there is, that life ends in silence and darkness. If I can find the secret of eternal life, I can defy the fate that took him."

Siduri's eyes softened, though her tone remained firm. "Do you think immortality will erase your grief? Or will it chain you to it, stretching your pain across an eternity?"

Gilgamesh's fists clenched on the table. "If immortality means I can protect those I love, then I will bear whatever burden it brings."

Siduri sighed, leaning back in her chair. "You speak with conviction, but have you thought of the cost? To be immortal is to stand apart, to watch as those you cherish fade while you remain. Life's beauty comes from its impermanence. Its fleeting nature gives each moment weight."

Gilgamesh shook his head, his voice rising with frustration. "Then why must we suffer? Why must the gods give us love only to take it away?"

For a moment, Siduri said nothing, her gaze flickering to the fire. When she spoke, her voice was quiet but resolute. "Because it is in loss that we find meaning. The love you shared with Enkidu does not vanish with his death. It shapes you. Without the pain of his loss, would you be here now, searching for answers?"

Gilgamesh stared at her, the weight of her words settling over him like a shroud. The fire crackled in the silence, its light dancing across their faces. At last, he said, "I hear your words, but I cannot accept them. I must find Utnapishtim. I must know if there is a way to defy death."

Siduri studied him for a long moment, her expression a mixture of sadness and respect. "Then I will not stop you," she said. "But I will warn you that what lies ahead is not what you expect. Utnapishtim may have answers, but they may not be the ones you seek."

She rose and gestured toward the door. "Beyond this place lie the Waters of Death. To cross them, you will need the ferryman, Urshanabi. He is not easily persuaded, but if you can convince him, he will guide you."

Gilgamesh stood, inclining his head in gratitude. "Thank you," he said. "For your counsel and your kindness."

Siduri smiled faintly. "May your journey bring you the truth you seek, even if it is not the truth you desire."

As Gilgamesh stepped out into the cool night air, the sight of the Waters of Death stretched before him. It was a vast, still expanse of darkness that seemed to swallow the horizon. The wind carried the faint scent of decay, a reminder of the peril that lay ahead. Siduri's words echoed in his mind, a quiet refrain that warned of the trials to come.

He squared his shoulders and walked toward the shore. Somewhere across those waters, Utnapishtim waited, and with him, the answers that would either shatter or save him. The journey was far from over, but Gilgamesh knew he could not turn back. For Enkidu, for himself, and for the truth, he would face whatever lay ahead.

Chapter 27:

DRINKING AMONGST GODS

The first rays of dawn broke over the Waters of Death, painting the surface with streaks of muted gold and silver. Gilgamesh stood at the shoreline, his figure a silhouette against the ethereal glow of the rising sun. The water stretched endlessly before him, its surface unnervingly still, as though time itself had paused. The cool breeze carried with it the faint tang of salt and something deeper, a primordial stillness that seemed to watch him from the horizon.

His mind was heavy, filled with the weight of Siduri's words and the enormity of the journey still ahead. He clenched his fists, his resolve unbroken but fraying at the edges as doubts began to creep in. Would Utnapishtim truly hold the answers he sought, or was he chasing an illusion, a cruel hope dangled by the gods?

As the sun rose higher, the light grew brighter, and with it came a warmth that settled over him like a comforting hand. He turned his face to the sky, closing his eyes against the brilliance, and when he opened them again, he was no longer alone.

Shamash, the sun god, stood before him, his presence radiant and commanding. He was tall and broad, his golden armor catching the morning light and reflecting it in dazzling rays. His face, though stern, held a kindness that softened the sharp lines of his divine features. His eyes, glowing with an intensity that seemed to pierce through mortal pretenses, fixed on Gilgamesh with a mixture of amusement and concern.

"Well, Gilgamesh," Shamash said, his voice carrying the resonance of celestial authority tempered with the warmth of an old friend. "You've made it to the shore. I see the darkness hasn't swallowed you yet."

Gilgamesh blinked, momentarily caught off guard by the casual tone of the god's greeting. He inclined his head slightly, an acknowledgment of the divine presence before him. "Shamash," he said, his voice steady but tinged with weariness. "You honor me with your presence."

Shamash crossed his arms, the faintest hint of a smile playing at the corners of his mouth. "Honor you? Perhaps. Or perhaps I'm here because I can't bear to see a man as stubborn as you waste away chasing shadows."

Gilgamesh frowned, his brows drawing together. "I seek Utnapishtim," he said firmly. "He holds the secret to immortality. If there is even a chance to escape death, I must take it."

Shamash sighed, his gaze drifting to the horizon. "You mortals," he said softly, shaking his head. "Always so eager to defy what you cannot change. Do you not see the burden you carry, Gilgamesh? The grief, the fear, it consumes you, drives you to the edge of the world. And for what? To find a man who has been set apart by the gods, who lives not as you live, but in eternal isolation?"

Gilgamesh's jaw tightened, his fists clenching at his sides. "I cannot accept death as the end," he said. "I cannot stand by and watch those I love fade into nothingness. If Utnapishtim has the answer, I will find it."

Shamash turned his gaze back to Gilgamesh, his expression softening. "I know your heart, Gilgamesh," he said. "Do you think I do not understand your grief? I have watched you since you were a child, watched you grow into the king of Uruk, watched the bond between you and Enkidu. I was with you when you faced Humbaba, when you slew the Bull of Heaven. And I was with you in the Path of Darkness."

Gilgamesh's eyes widened slightly, surprise breaking through his composure. "You… you were with me?"

The god nodded. "I lengthened the day," he said simply. "I held the sun's course to ensure you had enough time to make it through. Do you think the darkness relents for mortals? It would have swallowed you whole without my aid."

The revelation stunned Gilgamesh into silence. He looked away, his gaze falling to the still waters of the sea. "Why?" he asked after a long moment. "Why would you help me if you think my journey is folly?"

Shamash smiled faintly, the warmth of it like the sun breaking through clouds. "Because, stubborn king, I am on your side. I see your pain, your determination, and I cannot help but admire it, even as I pity it. But I am here now to urge you to stop. To return to Uruk, to the life you still have. You do not need to go further."

Gilgamesh shook his head, his voice resolute. "I cannot stop. Not until I have the answers I seek."

The sun god regarded him quietly for a long moment, then sighed deeply. "Very well," he said. "If you must persist, then at least take a moment to rest. The journey across the Waters of Death is not one you can face without strength, and I am not ready to see you torn apart by your own folly."

Gilgamesh hesitated, his instincts urging him forward, but Shamash raised a hand. "Stay," the god said. "Just for one more day. Have some ale with me. Siduri will not forgive you for leaving her without drinking enough to make you sick."

A flicker of a smile crossed Gilgamesh's face despite himself. "You jest, Shamash?"

The god's grin widened. "Perhaps. But Siduri would be the

first to call you a rude guest. And she brews the finest ale this side of the Waters of Death. What harm is there in one more day? You've already come farther than most."

Gilgamesh let out a long breath, his shoulders relaxing slightly. "One day," he agreed. "But no more."

Shamash clapped him on the shoulder, his touch light but imbued with an otherworldly energy. "Good," he said. "Let us sit and drink while the sun journeys across the sky. Even kings and gods deserve moments of respite."

The two sat near the shore, the gentle warmth of the sun casting a golden glow over the land. Gilgamesh sipped the ale that Siduri had made, the sweetness and richness soothing the frayed edges of his resolve. Shamash spoke of the world, of the mortals he watched, and even of Siduri herself, his words light and filled with humor.

For the first time in what felt like an eternity, Gilgamesh laughed. It was a brief reprieve, a flicker of light in the shadow of his grief. But as the day wore on and the sun began its descent, the weight of his journey returned. When Shamash rose to leave, his radiant form glowing against the fading light, Gilgamesh felt the pull of his purpose once more.

"Thank you, Shamash," he said, his voice quiet but sincere. "For your kindness, and for reminding me that even in the midst of sorrow, there is still light."

The god inclined his head, his expression one of quiet pride. "Go well, Gilgamesh," he said. "May your journey bring you the answers you seek, even if they are not the answers you expect."

With that, Shamash departed, his form dissolving into the horizon as the sun dipped below the sea. Gilgamesh stood alone once more. In his heart, there was a flicker of warmth. It was a reminder that even in the face of death, he was not entirely alone. Tomorrow, he would face the Waters of Death. But tonight, he allowed himself a moment of peace, the sun's warmth lingering on his skin like a whispered blessing.

Chapter 28:

THE FERRYMAN'S JEST

The Waters of Death stretched endlessly, the black surface unnaturally still and void of reflection. It seemed to absorb light rather than reflect it, creating an expanse so ominous that even Gilgamesh, for all his strength and determination, felt the weight of its presence. A cool mist hung in the air, carrying a faint metallic tang that clung to his skin and filled his lungs with unease.

At the shore, a boat lay tethered to a post. It was an ancient vessel, its hull weathered and blackened as if scorched by the very waters it floated upon. Standing beside it was a figure cloaked in shadow, his face hidden beneath a hood. His movements were deliberate, his posture calm but charged with authority. This was Urshanabi, the ferryman of the Waters of Death, tasked with guiding only those whose purpose warranted such peril.

Gilgamesh approached with a confidence he would not have had the previous day. Urshanabi turned to face him, his hooded gaze piercing despite the obscured light. His presence carried the weight of ages, an aura of wisdom and danger intertwined.

"You are bold to come here, mortal," Urshanabi said, his voice deep and resonant, echoing with an unearthly timbre. "Few dare approach the Waters of Death, and fewer still return. Who are you, and what madness drives you to seek passage across this cursed expanse?"

"I am Gilgamesh," the king replied, his tone steady despite the tension in the air. "King of Uruk, born of the gods and men. I seek Utnapishtim, the one who holds the secret of eternal life."

Urshanabi's head tilted slightly, his posture rigid but not hostile. "And why, Gilgamesh, do you seek what even the gods envy? What makes you believe you are worthy of such knowledge?"

Gilgamesh's voice faltered momentarily before his grief lent it strength. "Because I have lost my brother, Enkidu. Death claimed him, and I could do nothing to stop it. The gods have cursed us to lives as fleeting as shadows, but I will not accept that. If there is a way to defy death, I must find it."

Urshanabi studied him in silence, the hood of his cloak obscuring his face but failing to hide the intensity of his scrutiny. "The waters you wish to cross are no ordinary barrier," he said. "They are a test, a crucible. To touch them is to invite death itself. Even the gods tread carefully here. What makes you think you will survive?"

"I will survive because I must," Gilgamesh replied. "For Enkidu. For the truth. For the people who look to me as their king."

Urshanabi nodded slowly, a faint sound that could have been approval or regret. He gestured to the boat. "Then you will need these," he said, producing a bundle of strange, rune-carved stones and charms from beneath his cloak. "They are what allow this vessel to traverse the waters safely. Without them, you will be lost."

The sight of the charms, so intricately detailed and pulsating faintly with energy, filled Gilgamesh with a mixture of awe and frustration. They were symbols of his dependence, tools that reminded him of the limits of his own strength. His grief flared into anger, and before he could stop himself, he lashed out.

"No trinket determines my fate!" he roared, grabbing the stones and hurling them to the ground. They shattered upon impact, their fragments scattering across the rocky shore. The faint hum of their magic faded into silence, leaving a void that felt heavier than the air itself.

Urshanabi stood still, his posture unmoving, though his presence seemed to radiate disappointment. "You have done a foolish thing, king of Uruk," he said, his voice cold and unyielding. "Without those charms, this boat cannot cross the Waters of Death. You have sealed your own fate."

Gilgamesh froze, the weight of his impulsive act crashing over him like a wave. He clenched his fists, his face contorted with frustration. "Tell me what I must do," he demanded. "I will make this right."

Urshanabi tilted his head, his tone suddenly laced with dry humor. "Very well, Gilgamesh. You will cut down 120 trees from the surrounding forest and fashion them into punting poles. With each pole, you will push the boat forward, keeping yourself and the vessel from touching the water."

Gilgamesh's jaw tightened, but he nodded, turning toward the sparse forest that bordered the shore. He would not be deterred. For days, he toiled, cutting down the tallest trees he could find and stripping them of their branches. His muscles burned, his hands blistered, but he pressed on, his grief fueling his determination. By the time he had fashioned the poles, his body ached with exhaustion, but his resolve remained unbroken.

He returned to Urshanabi, the massive bundle of poles. Dropping them to the ground, he turned to the ferryman, his voice steady. "I am ready."

Urshanabi regarded him for a moment before chuckling softly. "You are nothing if not relentless," he said. "But there is no need for those poles. The boat can cross the waters without them."

Gilgamesh's eyes narrowed, his fists clenching. "You jest?" he growled.

"I do," Urshanabi replied, his tone light. "But the effort

was not wasted. You have proven your resolve, and that, perhaps, is worth more than the charms you so impulsively destroyed."

Gilgamesh's frustration simmered, but it was tempered by the faintest flicker of admiration for the ferryman's cunning. Without another word, he stepped onto the boat, his movements deliberate. Urshanabi followed, his oar in hand, and with a single, smooth push, the vessel began to glide into the abyssal waters.

The silence of the journey was reflective, broken only by the soft creak of the boat and the faint ripples of the water. Shadows shifted beneath the surface, their movements slow and deliberate, as though watching. The air grew colder, and an unnatural stillness pressed against Gilgamesh, but he kept his gaze fixed on the horizon, where the distant shore awaited.

"You have crossed into a realm where few mortals dare tread," Urshanabi said, his voice low. "What lies ahead will test not just your body but your spirit. Are you prepared for the truths you seek?"

Gilgamesh nodded, his voice firm. "I have come too far to turn back."

Chapter 29:

THE WATERS OF DEATH

The Waters of Death were an expanse of black so deep it seemed to swallow light, sound, and even thought. The air was dense and cold, pressing against Gilgamesh with a weight that felt unnatural. Every ripple on the water's surface seemed to carry menace, as though the waters themselves were alive, waiting to claim him at the first misstep. In the narrow boat, Urshanabi stood at the helm, his hooded figure like a specter against the dim glow of the horizon. His oar moved steadily, its runes glowing faintly with each stroke, cutting through the darkness with an unnatural grace.

The silence was oppressive, broken only by the rhythmic creak of the boat and the faint splash of the oar. Gilgamesh sat motionless, his hands gripping the edges of the vessel as his mind churned with memories and questions. The weight of Enkidu's loss, the fear of his own mortality, and the uncertainty of what lay ahead all tangled together, an unrelenting storm within him.

Urshanabi's voice broke the stillness, low and steady, carrying a tone of ancient wisdom. "King of Uruk, do you know the waters you now cross? They are more than a barrier. They are a reflection of the souls who have sought to defy their fates, a graveyard of forgotten dreams."

Gilgamesh looked up, his gaze meeting the shadowed face of the ferryman. "I do not care for their stories," he said, his voice firm

137

despite the cold. "I only care for the answers that lie ahead."

Urshanabi tilted his head, his movements deliberate. "And yet, their stories are a mirror to your own. Every soul that dared to cross these waters believed they could challenge the gods. Most met only despair."

Before Gilgamesh could reply, a shadow passed beneath the boat, vast and serpentine. The water rippled faintly, and the vessel rocked with a force that made Gilgamesh clutch the sides tighter. He peered over the edge, his eyes straining to make sense of the movement below.

"What was that?" he asked, his voice low but tense.

Urshanabi did not stop rowing. "That," he said, his voice reverent, "was Tiamat's child. The great Leviathan that swims in these cursed waters. A fragment of the chaos that once ruled the world."

Gilgamesh frowned, leaning slightly forward. "Tiamat? The mother of monsters?"

Urshanabi nodded, his gaze fixed on the water ahead. "Before the gods brought order to the heavens and the earth, there was Tiamat. She was the sea, the chaos, the primordial void. From her wrath came Leviathans such as the one you saw. When the younger gods rose and slew her, they scattered her essence across creation, but fragments remain. This beast, born of her power, guards these waters. It ensures that only the truly determined reach the other side."

The boat rocked again, harder this time, and a massive, coiling shadow rose just beneath the surface. For a moment, the great serpent breached, its shimmering black scales glinting faintly in the dim light. Its eyes, golden and unblinking, regarded the boat with an intelligence that sent a chill through Gilgamesh. Its maw opened slightly, revealing rows of jagged teeth, before it slipped back beneath the surface with barely a ripple.

Gilgamesh's breath caught in his throat, his pulse pounding. "And it does not attack?"

"It will," Urshanabi said calmly, "if you falter. The Leviathan senses weakness, fear, doubt. It is a reflection of the chaos within you. If you lose focus, if your resolve wavers, it will strike."

The words struck Gilgamesh with the weight of truth. He forced his breathing to steady, his grip to loosen. He could not afford to falter—not here, not now. "And what of you, ferryman?" he asked. "You cross these waters often. Does it not test you?"

Urshanabi chuckled softly, a sound that was neither warm nor cold. "I am of these waters, Gilgamesh. I am part of their balance. They do not test me as they test you. But that does not mean I am beyond their reach."

The boat continued forward, the Leviathan's shadow following just beneath, a silent reminder of the peril that surrounded them. Urshanabi's oar moved with an unbroken rhythm, and his voice, though low, carried the weight of ages.

"Tiamat's story is one of chaos and order, destruction and creation. The gods slew her because they feared her power, yet they used her body to shape the world. Her blood became the rivers, her bones the mountains, her tears the seas. But fragments of her chaos remain, reminders that order is never complete, that the gods' victory was not absolute."

Gilgamesh frowned, his thoughts turning inward. "And this Leviathan, does it serve the gods, or does it serve chaos?"

Urshanabi's gaze flicked toward him, his hooded face unreadable. "It serves itself. It is neither bound to the gods nor to chaos. It is a force of its own, much like you, king of Uruk."

The words hung in the air, their weight settling over Gilgamesh like a shroud. He thought of his own defiance, his refusal to accept the fate the gods had decreed for him and for Enkidu. Was he, too, a fragment of chaos, challenging the order of the world?

The thought both unsettled and emboldened him.

The boat rocked again, and Gilgamesh looked down to see the Leviathan's golden eyes staring up at him through the dark waters. They seemed to pierce into his very soul, as if measuring his worth. He did not look away, meeting the creature's gaze with unyielding determination. Slowly, the shadow beneath the water began to drift away, its massive form disappearing into the depths.

"You have passed its first test," Urshanabi said quietly, his voice carrying a note of approval. "But remember, Gilgamesh, these waters hold many trials. You will face them all before this journey ends."

The boat continued on, the silence once again pressing heavily upon them. The shore remained distant, shrouded in mist, but Gilgamesh felt a flicker of hope. He had come this far, endured so much. He would not falter now.

The Leviathan did not reappear, but its presence lingered, a reminder of the chaos that lay beneath the surface. As they approached the far shore, Urshanabi's voice broke the silence once more.

"Beyond this place lies Utnapishtim," he said. "The one who has seen the flood, who has walked with the gods. But know this, Gilgamesh, that the answers you seek may not bring you the solace you desire. The truths you uncover may weigh heavier than the grief you already carry."

Gilgamesh nodded, his resolve unshaken. "Then let them weigh. I will carry whatever burden is required to honor Enkidu, to understand what it means to live forever in the hearts of the people."

The boat scraped against the rocky shore, and Gilgamesh stepped out, his feet sinking into the damp earth. He turned to thank Urshanabi, but the ferryman and the boat were already gone, as if the waters had claimed them once more.

Alone, Gilgamesh stood at the edge of the unknown. The

mist began to part, revealing a winding path that led upward to a solitary hut perched atop a hill. Beyond it, the horizon stretched endlessly, a blend of light and shadow that seemed to mirror his own heart.

Taking a deep breath, he began to climb. Each step brought him closer to the answers he had sought for so long, and to the truths that would forever shape his journey. Behind him, the Waters of Death remained still, the Leviathan's shadow a faint, lingering presence beneath the surface, watching.

Chapter 30:

A MODEST HUT

The journey had led Gilgamesh through realms of peril and wonder, but as he stood before the modest hut of Utnapishtim, the culmination of his arduous quest, a sense of trepidation gnawed at him. The hut was unremarkable, its weathered wood and sagging roof offering no indication of the extraordinary being who resided within. Yet it exuded an aura of ancient power, an unassuming vessel for the wisdom and mysteries of the gods.

Gilgamesh adjusted his cloak, damp from the mists that clung to the shore, and stepped forward. Each movement was deliberate, his feet pressing into the soft earth with the weight of purpose. The stillness around him felt oppressive, as though the air itself was holding its breath. When he reached the threshold, he hesitated, his hand poised to knock. The faint crackle of a fire reached his ears, a quiet rhythm in the otherwise silent world.

Before he could strike the door, a voice called from within, calm and resonant, carrying an ageless authority. "Enter, Gilgamesh."

The sound of his name, spoken by one who had never met him, sent a shiver down his spine. He pushed the door open and stepped inside. The room was dim, lit only by the flickering fire in a small hearth. Shadows danced on the walls, their movements slow and deliberate, mirroring the unhurried passage of time in this timeless place.

Seated beside the fire was Utnapishtim. The man's presence was as unassuming as his home, but there was a gravity to him, a quiet power that filled the room. His face was lined with deep wrinkles, his hair a silver cascade that framed piercing eyes. Though his body showed the marks of age, his gaze was sharp and unyielding, as if it could see straight into Gilgamesh's soul.

"You are Gilgamesh," Utnapishtim said, his tone neutral but firm. It was not a question.

"I am," Gilgamesh replied, inclining his head slightly. "And you are Utnapishtim, the one who has conquered death."

Utnapishtim gestured to a simple wooden chair opposite him. "Sit, king of Uruk. You have come far, and your story carries the wear of a long journey."

Gilgamesh obeyed, lowering himself into the chair. For a moment, neither man spoke. The fire crackled softly between them, its light flickering in their eyes.

"You know why I have come," Gilgamesh said at last, his voice steady despite the turmoil within. "I seek the secret of immortality."

Utnapishtim leaned back slightly, his expression unreadable. "I do know. But tell me, Gilgamesh, why do you seek what even the gods do not wish for? Why do you, a mortal, dare to challenge the natural order?"

The question, though softly spoken, landed like a blow. Gilgamesh clenched his fists, his grief bubbling to the surface. "I have lost my equal, my friend, my beloved, Enkidu," he said, his voice thick with emotion. "Death claimed him, and I could do nothing. He was taken by the same fate that will one day claim us all. I refuse to accept this. There must be a way to defy it."

Utnapishtim regarded him in silence for a long moment, his gaze steady and piercing. "You speak of loss, of love," he said finally. "These are the bonds that make life worth living, and yet they are the very bonds you would sever with immortality. Tell me, Gilgamesh, what do you believe you will gain? Will eternal life restore what you have lost?"

Gilgamesh's jaw tightened, his voice rising with desperation. "If I can find the secret of immortality, I can protect those I love. I can spare others the pain I have endured. I can build a legacy that will never fade, a city that will stand forever, untouchable by the passage of time."

Utnapishtim shook his head slowly, a faint sigh escaping his lips. "You chase a mirage," he said, his tone tinged with sorrow. "Immortality is not the cure for grief, nor is it the shield you imagine. It is a burden, one that strips life of its meaning. Without death, there is no urgency, no reason to cherish the moments we have. To live forever is to drift, unanchored, through an endless sea of time."

Gilgamesh leaned forward, his hands gripping the edges of his chair. "You say this because you have it. You speak of burdens, but you were spared. You were chosen. How can you claim to understand my pain when you have escaped the fate that looms over every mortal?"

Utnapishtim's gaze grew sharper, his voice firm. "You think I was spared? You think I do not carry pain? Then listen, king of Uruk. Hear my story, and know the cost of what you seek."

For a moment, the room was silent except for the crackle of the fire. Gilgamesh stared at Utnapishtim, his mind churning with questions and emotions he could not name. The old man's words carried the weight of truth, but Gilgamesh's grief burned brighter, his desperation pushing him forward.

"I have crossed the wilderness," Gilgamesh said, his voice low but fierce. "I have faced beasts and gods, walked through the Path of Darkness, and sailed across the Waters of Death. All of it, for this moment, for the chance to learn from you. Do not deny me now. Tell me what you know."

Utnapishtim studied him for a long moment, his expression

unreadable. Then he nodded slowly. "Very well," he said. "I will tell you. But know this, Gilgamesh, that the answers you seek may not bring you peace. Sometimes, the truths we find are more painful than the questions we carry."

The fire flickered, its light casting shadows that seemed to shift and writhe. Utnapishtim leaned forward, his voice quiet but firm, carrying the weight of millennia. "Listen, and understand what it means to defy the gods."

Chapter 31:

THE TALE OF UTNAPISHTIM

Utnapishtim sat motionless, his face illuminated by the flickering firelight. The weight of his words seemed to settle over the small hut like a thick mist, and for a long moment, the only sound was the crackle of the flames. Gilgamesh, seated across from him, leaned forward, his expression a mixture of awe, frustration, and desperation. This was the moment he had fought so hard to reach, the tale he had braved the wilderness, darkness, and death itself to hear.

"In the days before the flood," Utnapishtim began, his voice even and deliberate, "the gods grew weary of humanity. The noise of our lives, the chaos of our existence, it angered them. Enlil, in his fury, decreed that all mortals should be destroyed. He sought to cleanse the world, to silence the clamor of humanity forever."

Gilgamesh frowned, his brow furrowing. "Why? What had humanity done to deserve such wrath?"

Utnapishtim's gaze did not waver. "Perhaps nothing. Perhaps everything. The gods do not see as we see, king of Uruk. To them, we are both their creations and their burdens. When Enlil made his decree, it was final. But not all the gods agreed with his decision."

He paused, his eyes drifting toward the fire as if gazing into the distant past. "It was Ea, the god of wisdom, who took pity on us. He came to me in a dream, his voice as clear as the rising sun. He warned me of the coming deluge and gave me instructions to prepare. He told me to help build a great boat, large enough to carry my family, my craftsmen, and pairs of every animal that walked the earth."

Gilgamesh leaned closer, his breath catching in his throat. "And you obeyed?"

"I obeyed without question," Utnapishtim said. "For seven weeks, I labored. Ea gave me precise measurements, and I followed them to the letter. The boat was sealed with pitch and bitumen, its walls strong enough to withstand the fury of the storm. I gathered all that I could. I had to have food, tools, the creatures of the field. When the sky began to darken, I brought my family aboard and sealed the door."

The old man's voice softened, tinged with sorrow. "And then the storm came. The heavens opened, and the earth itself trembled. Rain fell in torrents, drowning the land. Rivers swelled, forests were uprooted, and cities vanished beneath the rising waters. The winds howled like wild beasts, tearing at the mountains and sweeping away all that stood in their path. For forty days and nights, the storm raged, unrelenting, as if the gods sought not only to destroy humanity but to unmake the world."

Gilgamesh's chest tightened as he imagined the scene. It had been filled chaos, despair, and the utter annihilation. "And you? What did you feel as you watched the world fall?"

"I felt despair," Utnapishtim admitted. "Even within the safety of the boat, I could hear the cries of the dying, the wails of the world as it was consumed. It was a torment unlike any other, to know that we alone had been spared."

He fell silent for a moment, his gaze distant. "When the storm finally subsided, all was silent. The waters stretched as far as the eye could see, a vast, desolate sea where once there had been life. Our boat had endured, and it came to rest upon the peak of Mount

Nimush."

Utnapishtim's voice grew softer, more introspective. "I released a dove to search for land, but it returned, finding no place to rest. Then I released a swallow, and still, the waters remained. Finally, I sent a raven, and when it did not return, I knew the waters had receded. We opened the door and stepped out onto the mountain, the air heavy with the scent of salt and sorrow."

"And then?" Gilgamesh pressed, his voice low but insistent.

"And then I offered a sacrifice to the gods," Utnapishtim said, his voice steady but tinged with bitterness. "The scent of the offering rose to the heavens, and the gods descended to see what remained. Ishtar wept, lamenting the destruction of humanity, and the other gods joined her, their grief overwhelming. But Enlil was furious. He raged that I had survived along with three others who had built boats with Ea's warning, that humanity had not been entirely eradicated."

Gilgamesh's fists clenched at the injustice of it. "But it was not defiance. You followed the wisdom of Ea."

"Exactly," Utnapishtim said, his gaze sharp. "Ea defended me, castigating Enlil for his disproportionate punishment. He argued that my survival was not rebellion, but wisdom, an act of obedience to the gods' own decree. In the end, Enlil relented. He blessed me and my wife, granting us eternal life. But it was not a reward, Gilgamesh. It was a reminder to the power of the gods and their mercy, though that mercy was thin and bitter."

The room fell silent, the fire crackling softly between them. Gilgamesh sat back, his thoughts a whirlwind of emotion. "You were spared," he said finally, his voice low. "You were granted what I seek. Why, then, do you speak of it with such sorrow?"

Utnapishtim's expression darkened, his voice heavy with regret. "Because immortality is not the gift you believe it to be, Gilgamesh. It is a burden. I have watched the world change, seen empires rise and fall, and endured the deaths of everyone I have ever known or loved. The years stretch endlessly before me, and without the bonds that give life meaning, eternity is hollow."

Gilgamesh leaned forward, his voice rising with urgency. "But there must be a way to preserve what matters. A way to live without losing everything."

Utnapishtim shook his head slowly, his gaze unflinching. "Mortals are not meant to live forever. It is the brevity of life that gives it beauty. Each moment, each connection, carries weight because it will not last. Immortality strips that away. To live without an end is to live without purpose."

The fire flickered, casting shadows across Gilgamesh's face as his frustration mounted. "Then why grant it to you? Why give you this gift if it is such a curse?"

"To teach," Utnapishtim replied, his voice quiet but firm. "To show mortals that death is not a punishment, but a part of the natural order. The gods granted me eternal life not as a blessing, but as a lesson that the value of life lies in its impermanence."

The room fell into a heavy silence, the crackling fire the only sound. Gilgamesh stared into the flames, his thoughts a maelstrom of defiance, grief, and reluctant understanding. He had come so far, endured so much, yet the answers he sought eluded him still.

Finally, he looked up, his gaze meeting Utnapishtim's. "If what you say is true," he said, his voice steady despite the storm within him, "then what am I to do? How do I live, knowing that death will claim all I hold dear?"

Utnapishtim regarded him with a quiet intensity. "You live, Gilgamesh. You cherish the moments you have. You honor the bonds that define you. And when the time comes, you accept the end, not as a defeat, but as a part of the story. That is the truth you must learn."

For a long moment, Gilgamesh said nothing.

Chapter 32:

BREAD FOR THE LIVING

The fire in Utnapishtim's hut burned low, its flickering glow casting long shadows across the walls. The weight of the immortal's words lingered in the air, pressing down on Gilgamesh as he sat, silent and brooding. The lessons Utnapishtim had shared about life's impermanence and the burden of eternity churned in his mind, conflicting with the grief and determination that had driven him this far.

But Gilgamesh was not ready to abandon his quest.

Utnapishtim, seated across from him, studied the king with a calm yet penetrating gaze. He seemed to sense the defiance in Gilgamesh, the unyielding spirit that refused to accept his own mortality. Finally, Utnapishtim spoke, his voice quiet but firm.

"You seek to conquer death, Gilgamesh," he said. "But can you conquer yourself? Can you master the very forces that define what it is to be mortal?"

Gilgamesh frowned, his frustration mounting. "What do you mean?"

Utnapishtim gestured toward the mat where Gilgamesh sat. "Stay awake, Gilgamesh," he said. "For six days and seven nights. Show me that you can resist even the simplest of mortal needs. If you can defy sleep, a shadow of death, then perhaps you will understand the weight of what you seek."

The challenge struck Gilgamesh like a blow. Sleep was an inevitability, a need as natural as breath. But his pride flared at the implication that he might fail. He straightened, his jaw tightening. "I accept your challenge," he said. "I will not close my eyes."

Utnapishtim nodded, though his expression carried a faint sadness. He rose and moved to the hearth, retrieving supplies like flour, water, and a small bundle of herbs. Gilgamesh watched him, confused. "What are you doing?"

Utnapishtim glanced at him, his hands deftly mixing the ingredients. "Each day that you remain awake, I will bake a loaf of bread. We shall mark the passage of time, so there can be no question of your success or your failure."

Gilgamesh said nothing, his determination etched into his features. He shifted slightly on the mat, adjusting his posture to keep himself alert. His gaze fixed on the fire, and the minutes began to stretch into hours.

At first, he felt strong. His body, honed by years of battle and hardship, was accustomed to endurance. He counted the cracks in the walls, the flickers of the flames, anything to occupy his mind and keep the pull of sleep at bay. Utnapishtim worked quietly at the hearth, shaping the dough and placing the first loaf into the fire.

The scent of baking bread filled the hut, warm and comforting. It was a cruel contrast to the battle raging within Gilgamesh's mind. Time dragged on, and his thoughts began to wander. He thought of Enkidu, of their shared adventures, their laughter, and the bond that had been stronger than any force he had ever known. The memory of his friend's death was a sharp pang that cut through his resolve, but it also made his eyes heavy with sorrow.

The first loaf was set aside, its golden crust cooling on a small table. Utnapishtim sat quietly, watching as the king's head began to nod. "Do not close your eyes, Gilgamesh," he said softly, though there was no malice in his tone.

Gilgamesh jerked awake, shaking his head to clear the fog. "I am awake," he said, his voice rough.

But as the hours stretched into days, the battle became unbearable. His limbs grew leaden, his thoughts sluggish. The warmth of the fire and the rhythmic crackle of the flames seemed to lull him, pulling him deeper into the fog. The second loaf joined the first, then the third. Each time Gilgamesh closed his eyes for a moment, Utnapishtim quietly marked his failure, placing another loaf on the table.

By the fourth day, Gilgamesh could no longer fight the pull of sleep. His head drooped, and his breathing grew slow and steady as exhaustion overtook him. Utnapishtim watched silently, his expression unreadable. The fifth and sixth loaves were baked, their warm scent mingling with the cool night air.

On the seventh morning, Gilgamesh awoke with a start, his body stiff and his mind clouded. He sat upright, blinking rapidly, his heart sinking as he saw the neat row of loaves on the table. Utnapishtim sat beside them, his face calm but tinged with disappointment.

"You have slept, Gilgamesh," he said simply. "You could not conquer sleep, the smallest shadow of death. How, then, do you hope to conquer death itself?"

Gilgamesh's fists clenched, frustration and shame warring within him. "It was not my will that failed," he said. "It was my body. It betrayed me."

Utnapishtim shook his head. "Your body is what makes you mortal, Gilgamesh. It is your connection to this world, your vessel for all the joys and pains of life. To fight it is to fight yourself, and that is a battle no man can win."

The weight of Utnapishtim's words settled heavily over

Gilgamesh, but he was not ready to yield. He rose to his feet, his voice steady despite the ache in his chest. "Then tell me, Utnapishtim. Is there nothing left for me? Is there no way to hold back the tide of death?"

For a long moment, Utnapishtim was silent. Then he sighed deeply, his gaze fixed on the horizon beyond the hut. "There is one thing I can offer you," he said at last. "Beneath the Waters of Death grows a plant said to restore youth. It is no true immortality, but it may give you a fragment of what you seek. If you can retrieve it, you may find answers, though not the ones you expect."

Gilgamesh's eyes brightened with renewed resolve. "I will find it," he said. "For Enkidu, for my people, and for the answers I have sought."

Utnapishtim nodded as he gave instruction. After, his expression was tinged with sadness. "Be warned, Gilgamesh. The plant is not a solution, but a test. Whatever you find beneath those waters will reveal the truths you must face. None are meant to live after entering the water."

Stepping out into the cool night air in a hurry, Gilgamesh gazed toward the horizon where the sacred waters lay hidden. The stars above shimmered faintly through the mist, their light guiding him forward. He felt the weight of his journey settle once more upon his shoulders, but it did not deter him. The promise of the plant and the truths it held drove him onward.

Chapter 33:

THE LEVIATHAN'S SHADOW

The journey to the water's edge was fraught with trepidation, the weight of Gilgamesh's quest pressing down on him like the stones he would soon bind to his feet. The black expanse of the Waters of Death stretched endlessly before him, its surface unnaturally still, as though time itself had been swallowed within its depths. The air was cold, carrying a faint metallic tang, and the faint mist that clung to the shoreline swirled like restless spirits. Each ripple of the dark water seemed to beckon him forward and warn him away in the same breath.

Gilgamesh stood at the edge of the shore, his breathing steady but labored, his heart pounding in anticipation. The plant that Utnapishtim had described was no mere treasure. It was the culmination of his journey, a fragment of the immortality he had sought for so long. The sacred plant lay hidden beneath these cursed waters, its tendrils swaying in the unknown depths, guarded by forces that few mortals could comprehend and fewer still could survive.

He crouched on the rocky shore, binding heavy stones to his feet with strips of leather. His hands worked methodically, the muscle memory of his warrior's training taking over even as his mind raced. The stones were rough, their surfaces scratching his skin, but they would serve their purpose, to anchor him to the depths and allow him to walk on the seabed. Beside him, a coil of rope lay ready, a lifeline to the world above should his strength falter.

The preparation gave him time to reflect, though his thoughts were turbulent. He thought of Enkidu, of the bond they had shared and the loss that had driven him to this place. He thought of Utnapishtim's words, both cautionary and cryptic, and of the challenge that lay before him. The Leviathan's shadow loomed large in his mind, a beast born of chaos and ancient wrath. Gilgamesh clenched his jaw, forcing himself to push the fear aside. He had faced gods, monsters, and the wrath of nature itself. He would face this as well.

With the stones secured, he stood and took a deep breath, his gaze fixed on the dark water. The surface was unnervingly calm, reflecting the dim light of the distant stars. He wrapped the rope around his waist, tightening the knot with a firm tug. One last breath filled his lungs, and then he stepped into the water.

The cold hit him like a blow, stealing his breath and chilling him to the bone. The weight of the stones pulled him downward, his body sinking steadily into the abyss. As he descended, the light above grew faint, the surface blurring into a distant shimmer before vanishing entirely. The water pressed against him, heavy and suffocating, its silence oppressive. Each movement felt sluggish, as though the very water sought to resist his intrusion.

The depths were a realm of absolute darkness, the kind that seemed to swallow not only sight but sound and thought as well. Gilgamesh's heartbeat thundered in his ears, the only reminder of his life amidst the lifeless expanse. He kept moving, his feet finding grip on the uneven seabed. Each step sent a small plume of silt drifting into the water, the only evidence of his presence in this forgotten world.

Then, faintly, a light appeared in the distance, a soft, ethereal glow that pulsed gently like a heartbeat. Gilgamesh's chest tightened as he recognized it. It was the sacred plant. It grew alone in the vast expanse, its tendrils swaying as if moved by a breeze that did not exist. The glow illuminated the rocky floor around it, creating a small sanctuary of light in the otherwise impenetrable darkness.

He quickened his pace, the weight of the stones making each step a laborious effort. His lungs burned with the need for air, but he pressed on, his resolve unyielding. Finally, he reached the plant and knelt before it, his fingers trembling as they closed around its delicate stem. The plant felt alive in his grasp, its surface warm and faintly pulsing, as though it held the essence of life itself.

But as he turned to ascend, the water around him seemed to shift, the darkness growing heavier and more oppressive. A faint vibration rippled through the seabed, and then he saw a massive shadow passing overhead, its movements slow and deliberate. The Leviathan.

The creature's sheer size was staggering, its serpentine body coiling through the water like a force of nature. Its scales shimmered faintly, catching the dim light of the plant and casting eerie reflections across the seabed. Its eyes, glowing like twin orbs of molten gold, scanned the water with an intelligence that was both terrifying and ancient. The Leviathan was no mindless beast; it was a guardian, a predator born of chaos and wrath.

Gilgamesh froze, his body pressed low against the seabed, the plant clutched tightly in his hand. His heart pounded in his chest, each beat a deafening drum in the silence. He dared not move, his every muscle tense as the Leviathan drew closer. Its massive maw opened slightly, revealing rows of jagged teeth that seemed designed to rend both flesh and stone.

The water around him swirled as the Leviathan circled, its immense body creating currents that threatened to dislodge him from his hiding place. He pressed himself harder into the rocky floor, his body blending into the shadows. Time stretched endlessly, each second an eternity as the beast lingered, its golden eyes scanning the water.

Gilgamesh's lungs screamed for air, the need to surface becoming unbearable. He gritted his teeth, his vision beginning to blur as his body betrayed him. Still, he did not move, his survival instinct warring with his resolve. The Leviathan paused, its gaze lingering for a moment that felt like a lifetime. Then, slowly, it began to drift away, its massive form fading into the darkness.

As the shadow disappeared, Gilgamesh pushed himself off the seabed, his legs straining against the weight of the stones. The ascent was agonizing, his body fighting against the water and his own exhaustion. The light above grew brighter, the surface drawing closer with each desperate stroke. Finally, he broke through, gasping for air as he clawed his way toward the shore.

He dragged himself onto the damp earth, collapsing onto his back as the plant remained clutched tightly in his hand. His chest heaved with each ragged breath, his body trembling from the effort and the lingering fear. The stars above shone faintly, their light a comforting contrast to the suffocating darkness he had escaped.

For the first time in days, a faint smile crossed his lips. The plant was a fragment of immortality, a symbol of his determination and sacrifice. Yet, as he lay there, staring at the sky, Utnapishtim's words echoed in his mind, a quiet reminder that the truths he sought might not bring the solace he desired.

The Leviathan's shadow remained imprinted on his thoughts, a reminder of the peril he had faced and the fragility of his mortal existence. He had survived the depths and claimed the sacred plant, but the journey was far from over. The answers he sought lay not in the plant itself, but in the trials that awaited him and the truths he would have to confront.

For now, he rested, the plant glowing faintly in his hand, its light a fragile promise in the vast expanse of the unknown.

Chapter 34:

THERE AND BACK

The journey back to Utnapishtim's hut was strangely serene, a stark contrast to the turmoil of the Waters of Death and the encounter with the leviathan. As Gilgamesh trudged across the barren landscape, the oppressive darkness that had shrouded his path seemed to lift. The air grew lighter, warmer, carrying a faint, earthy scent that grounded him in the reality of his steps. The ground beneath his feet, which had felt like shifting sands on his journey out, was now firm and steady, as though the land itself acknowledged his triumph.

The Flower of Renewal was tucked securely in his pack, its faint glow emanating warmth even through the coarse material. Its presence was a reminder of both his strength and the fragility of the life it represented. Though he had fought for it, risked everything to claim it, the question of its true purpose loomed large in his mind.

When the small hut came into view, its unassuming silhouette against the muted horizon, Gilgamesh felt a strange mixture of relief and anticipation. This was the place where his quest had found new meaning, where his confrontation with mortality had been laid bare. Utnapishtim, the man who had challenged his every conviction, waited within, and Gilgamesh knew that his journey was not yet complete.

As he approached, he saw Utnapishtim seated by the fire

just outside the hut, his posture relaxed but his eyes sharp and knowing. The flickering flames cast long shadows that danced across the ground, their light revealing the faint lines of age and wisdom etched into the immortal's face. He glanced at Gilgamesh and then at the pack slung over his shoulder, his expression unreadable.

"You have returned," Utnapishtim said, his tone steady but carrying a note of acknowledgment. "And you have retrieved the Flower of Renewal. You have actually succeeded in this task."

Gilgamesh lowered the pack carefully, his movements deliberate. The weight of his achievement and the questions it carried hung heavily in the air. "I have," he said, his voice calm but edged with resolve. "But I do not yet understand what it means."

Utnapishtim leaned forward slightly, his gaze fixed on Gilgamesh. The faintest smile touched his lips, though it was not one of triumph or condescension. It was the smile of a man who had seen the weight of the questions Gilgamesh now carried and understood the struggle they represented. "That is the true test, Gilgamesh," he said softly. "The flower is not an answer, it is a question. Its purpose is not something I, or anyone, can tell you. You must decide what it means, what it is worth, and how it will shape the path you walk."

Gilgamesh frowned, his hand instinctively tightening on the pack's strap. The words stung, not because they were cruel but because they reflected a truth he was not ready to face. "I risked everything to retrieve it," he said, his voice low. "I faced death, and yet… it feels incomplete. What was the purpose of my journey if not to find an answer?"

Utnapishtim stood slowly, the firelight casting long shadows across his frame. "Every journey carries its own meaning," he said. "But the meaning is not found in the destination. It is found in what you bring back with you. The flower is a fragment of the truth you seek, but the answers lie within you."

Gilgamesh's jaw tightened, his mind racing. He thought of Enkidu, of the bond they had shared and the grief that had driven him to the ends of the earth. He thought of Uruk, the great city he had built, its walls a testament to his strength and ambition. And he thought of the people who looked to him for guidance, their lives brief and fragile, yet filled with meaning. Slowly, the tension in his shoulders eased.

"I will take it back to Uruk," he said finally, his voice steady but tinged with uncertainty. "Perhaps it will help my people. Perhaps it will remind them, and me, of the strength we can find in the face of loss."

Utnapishtim inclined his head, his expression one of quiet respect. "A wise choice, Gilgamesh. You have learned much, but your journey is far from over. The truths you seek are still ahead, waiting to be uncovered. You have faced the waters, the shadows, and the beast, but the greatest trial lies not in the world beyond. It lies within."

The words settled over Gilgamesh like a mantle, heavy but grounding. He rose, his movements deliberate, the pack containing the Flower of Renewal slung securely over his shoulder. He met Utnapishtim's gaze, his expression one of gratitude and determination. "Thank you," he said, his voice firm. "For your wisdom and for your guidance."

Utnapishtim nodded, his eyes glinting with something that could have been pride or sorrow. "Go well, Gilgamesh," he said. "May your steps be steady, and may you find the truths you seek, even if they are not the answers you expect. The ferryman has arrived."

As Gilgamesh turned to leave, the fire crackled behind him, its light casting long shadows that seemed to stretch toward the horizon. The Flower of Renewal, warm against his back, was a reminder of the journey he had undertaken and the trials he had endured. Yet it was also a question, a fragment of a truth that would shape the path ahead.

Chapter 35:

LOST LOVE

The sun hung low in the sky as Gilgamesh approached Siduri's modest dwelling once more, its worn exterior a sharp contrast to the memories he carried from his first visit. This time, the air was lighter, the oppressive weight of his quest tempered by the flower he carried in his pack. The glow of its petals, faint but steady, had become a symbol of his endurance and a reminder of the trials he had faced. Yet, as he neared the alewife's home, he found himself filled with a strange sense of anticipation. Something unspoken lingered in the space between them, a truth yet to be revealed.

The door creaked open before he could knock, and Siduri stood in the threshold, her expression both surprised and resigned. She wore the same simple robes, her braided hair catching the warm hues of the fading sun. Her sharp eyes swept over him, lingering briefly on the pack slung over his shoulder.

"You return, King of Uruk," she said, her voice calm but tinged with curiosity. "I had wondered if I would see you again."

"I have crossed the Waters of Death," Gilgamesh replied, stepping forward. "And now I come to you, not as a seeker, but as one who has found… something."

Siduri's lips curved into a faint smile, though her eyes remained guarded. "Something is often more than nothing, and far less than everything. Come, Gilgamesh. Share a drink with me and tell me of your journey."

She stepped aside, and he entered the familiar warmth of her home. The scent of roasted grains and honeyed ale filled the air, mingling with the faint tang of sea salt. The fire in the hearth crackled softly, casting golden light across the room. Siduri moved to a low table, where two clay cups and a jug of ale sat waiting.

Gilgamesh took a seat across from her, setting his pack down carefully. He watched as she poured the ale, her movements steady and practiced. "Your home is as I remember it," he said. "A sanctuary amidst the chaos."

Siduri handed him a cup, her smile softening. "It is a place where travelers find a moment of peace, even if their journeys demand otherwise. And what of you, Gilgamesh? What have you found across the waters?"

He recounted his journey from the meeting with Utnapishtim, the encounter with the Leviathan, and the moment he grasped the Flower of Renewal from the depths. Siduri listened intently, her expression shifting between awe, sorrow, and quiet understanding. When he finished, she took a long sip of her ale and set the cup down gently.

"You have endured much," she said. "And you have claimed what few have ever touched. But what do you believe this flower will bring you?"

Gilgamesh hesitated, his fingers tightening around his cup. "It is a fragment of immortality," he said. "A piece of what I sought. Perhaps it will give meaning to the loss I have endured."

Siduri's gaze grew distant, her fingers tracing the rim of her cup. "Immortality is a weight, Gilgamesh," she said softly. "It is not what you imagine it to be."

Her words carried a note of personal pain that Gilgamesh could not ignore. He leaned forward, his brow furrowing. "You speak as one who knows," he said. "You have lived here for so long, offering solace to those who pass through. But who are you, Siduri? What brought you to this shore?"

She looked at him then, her eyes glinting with something that was both sorrow and resolve. "I was a survivor of the flood," she said. "Like Utnapishtim, I was granted eternal life. The gods decreed that I would remain here, on this side of the Waters of Death, while he was set apart on the far shore."

Gilgamesh stared at her, his breath catching. "You are his wife."

Siduri nodded, a faint, bitter smile playing on her lips. "Yes. I was with him on the boat, standing by his side as the storm consumed the world. We survived together, only to be separated by the gods' decree. For all eternity, we live on opposite shores, never to touch, never to share in the lives we once knew."

The weight of her revelation settled over the room, and Gilgamesh felt a pang of empathy that cut through his own grief. "Why would the gods do such a thing?" he asked. "To grant you life, only to condemn you to separation?"

Siduri's smile turned wry. "Because the gods delight in their paradoxes, Gilgamesh. They grant immortality not as a blessing, but as a reminder of their power and the cost of defiance. We are their symbols, their lessons for those who dare to challenge the natural order."

For a moment, neither of them spoke. The fire crackled softly, its light dancing across the walls. Then Siduri poured another round of ale, raising her cup. "To what remains," she said. "To the bonds we carry, even across impossible distances."

Gilgamesh raised his own cup, his voice low but steady. "To Enkidu," he said. "And to the strength that carries us forward."

They drank in silence, the ale warm and comforting. Gilgamesh studied Siduri as she sat across from him, her composure masking a depth of pain that mirrored his own. Her story was one of endurance, of finding purpose in the face of loss, and it resonated with him in a way he had not expected.

"You could leave," he said after a moment. "You could cross the waters and be with him."

Siduri shook her head, her expression gentle but firm. "The waters are not mine to cross, Gilgamesh. My place is here, offering respite to those who seek the far shore. It is the role I have been given, and I have come to accept it."

Her words lingered in his mind, a reminder of the truths Utnapishtim had spoken. Immortality was not a gift, but a burden, a lesson in the fragility and beauty of the mortal life he still carried.

As the night deepened, the two shared more stories, their conversation flowing like the ale in their cups. Siduri spoke of the life she had lived before the flood, of the simple joys she and Utnapishtim had shared, and of the grief that had shaped her resolve. Gilgamesh, in turn, spoke of Uruk, of its mighty walls and vibrant streets, and of the bond with Enkidu that had defined him.

When the fire burned low and the first light of dawn crept over the horizon, Gilgamesh rose to leave. Siduri stood with him, her expression calm but tinged with sadness. "Your journey is not yet over," she said. "But you carry more now than you did before. Perhaps that is enough."

He nodded, his grip tightening on the strap of his pack. "Thank you, Siduri," he said. "For your wisdom, your hospitality, and your strength."

She smiled, her eyes shining faintly in the firelight. "May your steps be steady, Gilgamesh. And may you find the peace that seeks your heart."

Chapter 36

THE SERPENT OF DECEPTION

Gilgamesh made his way back through the Garden of the Gods with measured steps, his every sense alive to the hush of this eternal twilight realm. The colorless sky above him seemed locked in a perpetual dusk, its pale light casting long shadows across the landscape. Vast trees with trunks of shimmering silver towered overhead, their leaves whispering secrets with the faintest breeze. Streams of water, impossibly clear, meandered between the tree roots, their surfaces reflecting the glimmer of starlight that seemed to emanate from nowhere and everywhere at once. It was a place that defied ordinary understanding, where beauty and mystery coexisted in delicate balance.

He clutched his prize close, the Flower of Renewal securely wrapped in a piece of cloth and nestled in his pack. Its faint glow, a gentle warmth that pulsed against his back, reassured him that his sacrifice in the depths of the Waters of Death had not been in vain. The memory of his struggle with the leviathan lingered—a brush with annihilation, saved only by his will to endure. Though he had emerged victorious, the reminder of the leviathan's golden eyes, ancient and unblinking, haunted him still. In those eyes, he had glimpsed a chaos older than any mortal memory.

Each step now felt lighter, unburdened by the suffocating dread that had shadowed him before. The knowledge that he carried a piece of immortality, albeit a fragile and uncertain one, lent him a calm determination. He was doing this for Uruk, for Enkidu, and for the promise of life that transcended the finality of death. Even if it provided only a glimpse of hope, the flower signified something worth fighting for.

He walked on, crossing a narrow bridge of living wood that bent and curved over a trickling stream. The faint, melodious notes of unseen birds echoed through the grove, a gentle chorus that lulled his mind and soothed his spirit. The air smelled of nectar and distant rain, a fragrance so sweet it was almost intoxicating. This was a realm that beckoned one to forget pain and sorrow, inviting them to lose themselves in its eternal serenity. Gilgamesh, however, was too disciplined to succumb to such illusions. He had not crossed the Waters of Death to abandon his sense of purpose in a paradise of half-truths.

Yet as he passed beneath a canopy of glimmering leaves, he felt an odd prickling at the back of his neck. A foreboding sense of being watched rose within him, an echo of the same primal awareness he had felt deep underwater. He froze, his breath catching in his throat. For an instant, the garden's hush intensified, and the gentle breeze seemed to stall. Gilgamesh turned slowly, scanning the foliage around him, but saw only the soft luminescence of the plant life and the gently rippling streams.

With a wary shake of his head, he continued onward. The hush lifted, and the breeze resumed, carrying with it the faint hum of insects. A sense of relief washed through him, but the tension in his muscles refused to ease entirely. Something about this place, with the intangible hush beneath the birdsong, the intangible watchfulness in the shifting leaves, unsettled him.

He paused at a crystal-clear pool that shimmered with internal light. Kneeling by its edge, he set his pack gently on the ground, still keeping one hand near it protectively. The water looked so pure, like melted starlight, that he felt compelled to drink. But caution overrode thirst. He remembered all too well how illusions and seductions could be laced through even the most benign-seeming corners of the Garden. Instead, he splashed some water on his face, letting the coolness center his mind.

Standing once more, he hefted his pack. The Flower of Renewal's faint glow pulsed gently through the cloth, a rhythmic comfort that matched his heartbeat. He spoke softly to Enkidu, as he had so many times in silent prayer. "I have done this for you," he murmured, voice trembling just enough to betray his grief. "For us. For the bond we shared. If there is a way to bring a part of you back, or to honor you in life beyond what the gods decreed, then I will find it."

A gentle rustling in the undergrowth drew his attention away from his reverie. Gilgamesh straightened, hand drifting toward the hilt of his sword. His eyes darted to the source of the noise, and from the tall grass emerged a serpent. At first, it appeared as another wonder of the Garden, for its scales shone with an emerald sheen, flecked with gold that caught and fractured the perpetual twilight into flecks of dancing light. It moved with a sleek, graceful glide that was mesmerizing to behold.

Yet Gilgamesh felt a chill run down his spine. There was something else, something far more sinister lurking beneath that glittering façade. The serpent's eyes were slitted and intelligent, reflecting the same ancient cunning he had seen in the Leviathan's golden gaze. It slithered closer, fixated on Gilgamesh's pack with an unmistakable hunger.

He felt his breath hitch, a sudden spike of dread. "Stay back," he warned, though his voice lacked the commanding authority he usually wielded. The serpent's only response was to flick its forked tongue, tasting the air with deliberate interest. Gilgamesh's gut twisted. This foul creature was drawn to the Flower of Renewal.

A flicker of recognition flared in his mind, a reminder of how mortals were not the only beings who desired immortality. The garden had many secrets, and no doubt many creatures prowled its fringes in search of what Gilgamesh now possessed. He took a step back, his feet sinking into the soft grass. His mind raced. If this serpent was drawn by the flower's power, what might it do?

Before he could act, the serpent coiled itself like a spring of living emerald, and with a sudden, precise strike, it sank its fangs into the leather pack. Gilgamesh let out a cry of alarm, lunging forward to snatch the bag away, but the serpent's coils tightened around the strap with a startling strength. In one fluid motion, it wrenched the pack from Gilgamesh's grasp, the cloth tearing as it slithered back through the grass, the precious flower in tow.

"No!" Gilgamesh roared, his voice echoing through the silent garden. He scrambled to his feet, heart pounding in his chest, and sprinted after the serpent. A surge of desperation fueled his limbs, the thought of losing the Flower of Renewal far more frightening than any beast he had faced thus far.

The serpent slithered with unnerving speed, its scales catching the golden light in a dazzling display. It darted between ancient trees, weaving effortlessly through the undergrowth. Gilgamesh followed in frantic pursuit, branches clawing at his arms, tall grass whipping at his legs. The once-serene beauty of the garden became a blur, overshadowed by the rising panic within him.

He pushed himself harder, muscles burning with exertion, his breath coming in ragged gasps. The serpent's golden scales flickered in and out of sight, guiding him deeper into the labyrinth of trees and vines. Every second felt precious, every heartbeat a mounting desperation. He could not lose the flower, not after all he had endured. Not after the risk, the heartbreak, and the final triumph over the depths of the Water of Death.

The chase seemed endless, a test of both Gilgamesh's willpower and the serpent's cunning. Finally, it slipped into a clearing, pausing at the base of a massive, ancient tree whose trunk soared into the twilight canopy. Gilgamesh burst into the clearing moments later, sword drawn, eyes wild with fury and fear. He spotted the serpent coiled at the tree's roots, his pack trapped between its glittering coils.

"Return it!" Gilgamesh demanded, voice breaking. He advanced cautiously, well aware that the serpent's strike could be fatal if laced with poison or the unnatural energies of the garden.

The serpent regarded him coldly, as though weighing the threat he posed. Then, with a slow, deliberate motion, it opened its maw. Gilgamesh watched in horror as it swallowed the Flower of Renewal whole, the faint glow of the blossom fading behind its emerald scales. A sudden, muted flash pulsed beneath the serpent's skin, then died away like a snuffed flame.

Gilgamesh stood frozen, his sword dangling uselessly in his grip. The realization that the precious flower, his one tangible hope for defying the gods, was gone, consumed, shattered him. The garden around him seemed to tilt, the quiet hum of unseen life replaced by the roar of his own blood in his ears.

"No," he whispered, voice hoarse with shock. "No!" he roared, his desperation exploding into a guttural howl. Rage and grief battered him in waves, twisting his heart in ways he had not thought possible. He staggered forward, sword raised, but the serpent was already slithering away, its body gleaming with renewed vigor. It slipped into the shadows between the trees, leaving Gilgamesh alone in the clearing, his blade lowered in defeat.

He sank to his knees, hands trembling against the damp earth. The emptiness in his chest was a tangible void, the meaning of his long journey eroded by a single, brutal moment. The faint rustle of leaves mocked him, as though the garden itself disapproved of his despair. Tears pricked his eyes, the weight of his labored breaths carving a hollow space in his chest. He had won the flower only to lose it to a creature that possessed no concept of empathy or justice.

Why? The unspoken question burned in his mind like a brand. Why permit him to succeed in retrieving the flower, only to have it stolen by a serpent? Was this yet another lesson of the gods, a demonstration of how fleeting mortal triumphs could be? He thought of Enkidu's face, the memory cutting through him like a blade. He had done it for his friend so that no more good men would die under a capricious fate.

Yet here he was, with nothing.

Time stretched into an interminable hush, the quiet patter of tears upon the soil all that remained of Gilgamesh's resolve. Eventually, the rush of emotions receded, leaving a hollow calm. He recalled Utnapishtim's cautionary words that the flower was not a solution but a test. With or without it, Gilgamesh remained the same mortal, bound by the same fleeting life. The flower might have granted him a fleeting restoration, but was that the immortality he truly sought?

Slowly, Gilgamesh rose, wiping away the evidence of his tears. A deep breath quaked through his chest, but a resolve glowed faintly in his eyes. A single thought crystalized in his mind, that despite losing the flower, his journey was not for nothing. The knowledge he had gained, the truths he had confronted, were real and lasting. The serpent's theft did not obliterate the lessons learned in the depths, nor the resilience he had discovered within himself.

Steadying himself, he looked around the clearing. The tranquil beauty of the garden reasserted itself, as if it had only paused to witness his sorrow. The delicate blooms, the shimmering leaves, the hidden streams all remained, unperturbed by mortal grief. In that moment, Gilgamesh felt the fragile equilibrium of the world around him, the interplay of life and death, triumph and loss.

He recalled the serpent's eyes, that gleam of malevolence far older than any mortal empire. The creature had stolen the flower, but not Gilgamesh's spirit. If anything, the theft underscored the ephemeral nature of victories, the constant demand that each day be lived with heart and purpose.

A faint smile tugged at Gilgamesh's lips, bittersweet but genuine. He sheathed his sword, acknowledging that force alone could not reclaim what was lost. The serpent was part of this place, bound to the garden's mysteries in ways he could not understand. He felt a flicker of gratitude that the creature had not slain him outright.

Perhaps there was some cosmic balance at play, an unspoken pact to let each other exist.

He spoke softly into the clearing, as if Enkidu, or even the gods, might hear. "I have lost the flower, but not the truth of my journey. I carry it still, in memory and in heart. Let this be enough for now."

With that, he turned back the way he had come, forging a path through the blossoming wonder of the garden. The hush of the twilight realm enveloped him once more, but it felt different now, less a sanctuary of possibility and more a realm of acceptance. He had no flower to protect him from fate, but he carried the intangible gifts of wisdom and resilience.

Step by step, he left the clearing behind. Streams babbled, their gentle song weaving through the hush. Birds of iridescent plumage took flight, trailing luminescent feathers that melted into the air. Each wonder he passed was a reminder that while the gods might shape the grand arcs of life, mortal hearts could still dare to dream, to love, and to hope.

He paused at a small footbridge, leaning against the vine-laden railing to catch his breath. The memory of the serpent's gleaming scales replayed in his mind. It was no ordinary beast, but a symbol—like so many trials in the garden, it was part of the tapestry that underscored the fragile boundary between hope and loss. Gilgamesh thought of Siduri's wise counsel, of Shamash's fleeting guidance, and of Utnapishtim's caution that immortality could be a burden rather than a gift.

Returning to the archway that marked the garden's boundary, Gilgamesh hesitated, glancing back at the tapestry of golden light and blossoming wonders. He felt no anger toward the garden for this final betrayal. Instead, he was reminded that the quest he had undertaken was never about grasping a single object to defy the gods. It was about confronting the nature of life itself, and in that confrontation, finding meaning beyond the illusions of invincibility.

He stepped through the arch, the brilliance of the garden receding behind him. Ahead lay the open path, leading back to the ferry crossing or perhaps to another unknown horizon. The weight of the serpent's theft lingered, but so did the knowledge that the true treasure lay within him. It was a newfound understanding that life's transience was, in fact, its greatest gift.

His footsteps carried him forward, each stride an affirmation of his humanity. Though battered by grief and disappointment, he walked on, forging a future that belonged to him alone. The serpent's cunning had stolen the Flower of Renewal, but it had not stolen Gilgamesh's resolve, nor had it erased the bond he shared with Enkidu.

In the distance, the faint glow of the setting sun painted the sky in lilac and gold, casting the world in tender hues. Gilgamesh looked up, inhaling a deep breath of the warm air. The path ahead might be long, the trials unceasing, but he would continue onward not simply in pursuit of immortality, but in pursuit of the love, hope, and heritage that defined a mortal life.

And so, with eyes turned to the horizon, Gilgamesh, King of Uruk, left the garden behind. The serpent that had slithered away into the shadows was as much a part of his story now as Enkidu, as Siduri, and as Utnapishtim. Each, in their own way, had shaped his journey. Each was a reminder that no victory was final, no sorrow total. Bound to time's relentless flow, Gilgamesh walked on, heart unbroken even in defeat, for he carried in his soul the one treasure that could never be stolen. It was the resolve to face the gods on his own terms, and to live, truly live, despite the sting of death that awaited all mortals.

Chapter 37:

THE SIEGE OF THE HEART

Gilgamesh made his way homeward with a heavy heart, the Garden of the Gods far behind him. The serpentine paths of that hallowed realm gave way to sun-scorched plains and stony hills, the tranquil hush replaced by a harsher wind that scoured the land. Though his journey had not yielded the everlasting life he had once sought, it had granted him a deeper awareness of the fragile beauty inherent in mortal existence. He carried neither immortal flower nor cosmic boon, only the quiet resolve that his struggles were not in vain. Even so, as he drew closer to Uruk, an anxious knot of foreboding coiled in his stomach.

He trudged through the final stretches of the plains, each step stirring up clouds of fine dust that clung to his worn tunic made of animal skins. The midday sun glared overhead, and though sweat beaded on his brow, he pressed on, fueled by a yearning to see his city once more. He imagined Uruk's towering walls rising from the horizon, the sight of them a balm to his weary soul. Yet, something felt amiss. The wind carried not the lively hum of commerce, nor the distant echoes of a bustling metropolis. Instead, there was a tense stillness, a held breath that made the hairs on the back of his neck stand on end.

At last, he crested a small rise and halted, his heart lurching at the sight before him. Uruk's magnificent walls built under his

175

direction, were intact, but below them stretched a sea of tents, a gathering of soldiers that ringed the city like a tightened noose. Smoke rose from scattered campfires, and the faint clank of armor and hum of voices drifted on the wind. Gilgamesh tensed, realizing that his kingdom was under siege.

He descended the rise quickly, his mind racing. Who would dare besiege Uruk, the city of mighty walls and proud defenders? It must be a substantial force, for few would challenge the defenses he had built and the renown of his people. Approaching with caution, he skirted the edges of the enemy camp, taking care not to draw attention to his lone figure. The tang of cooking fires and the pungent scent of sweat and horses hung in the air. He crouched behind a hill, peering through the heat-shimmer to count banners and arms. Fear and anger warred within him, stirring to life his protective instincts. He had left in pursuit of answers about mortality, and in his absence, a foe had come for his people.

Straining his ears, he caught snatches of conversation from the passing soldiers. They were men clad in battered leather and carrying spears or bows. They spoke in hushed, eager tones about the plan for the next assault, about the walls of Uruk, about the rumored return of its legendary king. Gilgamesh's brows knitted as he picked up the name of their leader, King Akka of Kish. The mention of Akka sent a jolt through him, for he recalled their last encounter, years ago, when Gilgamesh was young, brash, and supremely confident in his divine blood. He had crossed paths with Akka during a dispute over trade routes and water rights, and in his arrogance, he had insulted the man publicly. Gilgamesh had thought little of it at the time, sure that his might overshadowed any potential retribution. But now, it seemed, the old slight had come back to haunt him with a vengeance.

Keeping to the shadows, Gilgamesh slipped past the outer edges of the camp. He yearned to stride openly through the ranks, sword in hand, announcing his return. But rashness now could jeopardize the city, and in his wisdom gained from adversity, he understood stealth was the better choice. He needed to reach

Uruk's gates, to rally his people and learn the extent of this threat before confronting Akka head-on. Beneath the open sky, he felt the scorching sun on his neck, a reminder of the harshness of reality and the precarious hold of mortal achievements.

The city gates loomed up ahead, guarded by a small contingent of archers who peered anxiously over the battlements. Gilgamesh slipped toward a less-patrolled section of the wall, finding the secret entrance known only to a few. It was a discreet postern gate near the river, originally built for scouting parties. Slipping inside, he discovered the city under a weight of tension he had never felt before. The streets were unnervingly quiet, doors and windows shut tightly. The usual cacophony of Uruk's markets was reduced to a dull murmur, as if everyone waited, hearts clenched, for the next onslaught.

He pressed deeper into the city, crossing abandoned plazas and passing shuttered stalls. A hush lay over Uruk, broken sporadically by the clang of blacksmiths' hammers forging weapons or the distant cry of an anxious child. His chest tightened at the sight of farmers gathering behind walls, mothers clutching children, watchful warriors sharpening blades. This was not the confident metropolis he had left behind. Fear weighed on every stone.

Eventually, he reached the central square, where a small group of armed men had gathered around a fire. At their head was a seasoned soldier named Arumak, a man Gilgamesh recognized from earlier campaigns. The warrior's gaze shot up as Gilgamesh strode into the torchlight, his clothing dusty and tattered, his face etched with the lines of journey and grief.

"My king?" Arumak said, surprise and relief mingling in his voice. "You have returned?"

Gilgamesh placed a steady hand on the man's shoulder. "I have. Tell me what has happened. Why does Kish besiege our walls?"

Arumak's eyes flashed with anger. "They came two moons ago, led by King Akka. He claims you once insulted him, and that the only restitution is the surrender of Uruk's wealth, or your head. We have held them off so far, but the city grows weary. Food is scarce, morale is fragile. We needed you, my king."

Guilt washed through Gilgamesh, mingled with outrage. He had left to seek immortality, never suspecting his youthful arrogance might return to imperil his city. "I will speak with Akka," he said, though he knew the man's pride might make negotiations futile. "And if words fail, we will show him the might of Uruk."

Arumak nodded, though his expression was shadowed. "We stand ready, sire. But you should know that many have lost hope. They fear the gods are against us."

Gilgamesh's gaze hardened. He thought of the trials he had endured, of Utnapishtim's cautionary words about the futility of fighting fate. Yet here he was, forced to defend his people from a very mortal threat. "Then we remind them of our strength," he said. "Rally the warriors. I will not permit Kish to subjugate Uruk."

As evening deepened, Gilgamesh made his way through the city's quieter streets. Whispers spread rapidly of his return, and pockets of citizens emerged from their homes, eyes wide with a mixture of relief and awe. Though exhausted, Gilgamesh forced himself to greet them, to show them that their king had not abandoned them. When at last he allowed himself a moment's respite, he found that his feet had carried him to an old courtyard near the palace, a place where he and Enkidu had once sparred beneath the midday sun, their laughter echoing off sandstone walls.

The memory came unbidden, and a pang of loss cut through him. But now, he also felt a flicker of resilience. He had survived the water's depths, faced the leviathan, and learned great lessons from Utnapishtim and Siduri. The threads of his destiny were intertwined with Uruk's, and he would stand firm against any threat, mortal or divine.

Morning came shrouded in tension. Gilgamesh summoned the city's council that consisted of a group of elders, warriors, and advisors that would help lay out his plan. The immediate goal was to assess the enemy's strength and, if possible, speak to King Akka to avert further bloodshed. Some argued that vengeance for the siege was necessary, but Gilgamesh tempered their fervor, mindful that pride alone had sparked this conflict before.

A small delegation, bearing white banners, set forth from Uruk's gates. Gilgamesh, now in robes of purple and gold, walked at its head, sword at his side, cloak trailing in the dust. The air crackled with expectancy as they crossed the no-man's-land that stretched between Uruk's mighty walls and the ring of tents. Enemy archers watched their approach, bows half-drawn, but no arrow flew yet. A hush fell over both camps as Gilgamesh advanced, a hush broken only by the rustling of the Kish banners in the faint morning breeze.

At the center of the encampment, a large pavilion flew Kish's sigil. It was a stylized bull, rampant and fierce. Standing before it, flanked by armored guards, was King Akka himself. He was tall and broad-shouldered, his face set in a stern, unyielding scowl. Gilgamesh recognized him at once, though the years had added lines to his brow and a streak of silver to his hair.

"So," Akka said, his voice rumbling like distant thunder, "the king of Uruk returns at last. Have you come to surrender? Or do you merely want to see the ruin I have prepared for your city?"

Gilgamesh lifted his chin, meeting Akka's gaze without flinching. "I have come to speak, Akka," he said. "Our people need not suffer for a slight I gave you in my youth."

Akka's scowl deepened, anger flashing in his eyes. "You demean me still by calling it a mere slight, Gilgamesh. You humiliated me before my own men, mocked my lineage and my city. That scorn festered for years, and now I stand here with an army to reclaim my honor."

A faint trace of regret flickered across Gilgamesh's features. He remembered the incident. The brash, younger Gilgamesh, drunk on his own divine heritage, had disparaged Kish and its king. At the time, it seemed no more than a moment's bravado, a demonstration of his pride. But time had turned that moment into a wound that fueled Akka's vendetta.

"I was foolish then," Gilgamesh acknowledged. "I have learned much since. We can settle this without bloodshed. My people have no desire for war, nor do we thirst for Kish's destruction. Lay down your arms, and I will pay restitution for my insult."

Akka laughed, a harsh, mirthless sound. "You think gold and apologies will soothe years of scorn? You think to buy me off as one would buy a dog's loyalty? No, Gilgamesh. I will not be placated. I want you on your knees, stripped of your throne, so that Uruk may bow before Kish."

A chill ran through Gilgamesh, but his voice remained steady. "I will not kneel to you, Akka. Nor will I sacrifice Uruk to your pride. If it is a fight you want, I will defend my city."

Their eyes locked, neither man yielding. The hush around them was thick with tension, an entire army poised on a knife's edge between talk and battle. Finally, Akka turned sharply, signaling for his guards. "You have one day, Gilgamesh," he said coldly. "Surrender, or watch Uruk burn."

With that, the negotiations ended. Gilgamesh spun on his heel, leading his delegation back toward the gates. His mind raced, replaying the conversation. There would be no easy truce. Akka's pride and anger were as implacable as a tempest. Gilgamesh's only hope was to rally Uruk's defenders and find a strategy that could withstand Kish's might.

Night fell swiftly, bringing with it a grim hush broken by the occasional clash of distant patrols. From atop Uruk's walls, Gilgamesh surveyed the enemy camp. Fires glowed in the darkness, thousands of them dotting the plains like a field of burning stars. The scale of the siege was staggering, and for a moment, Gilgamesh felt the weight of his city's fate pressing on his shoulders. Memories of the flower he had lost, the illusions of immortality, flickered through his mind. What good was immortality if he could not save his city, his people, from the mortal threat that loomed?

Below him, the streets of Uruk were alive with frantic energy, soldiers arming themselves, smiths forging fresh weapons, and families gathering provisions. Gilgamesh descended into the heart of the city, mingling with the people he once believed were beneath his notice. Their fear was palpable, but so was their resolve. They had not forgotten how their king had built these towering walls, how he had defended them from monstrous forces. Despite their dread, they looked to Gilgamesh with hope shining in their eyes.

He joined a small gathering of captains in the palace courtyard, where an aging advisor named Makhir spread a crude map on a wooden table. By torchlight, they discussed the vulnerabilities of Uruk's gates, the strengths and weaknesses of Kish's forces, and the uncertain morale of Uruk's own defenders.

"Makhir," Gilgamesh said softly, "tell me, truly, how do our supplies stand? How many days can we hold before hunger gnaws at us?"

Makhir sighed, his lined face etched with worry. "We have enough grain and dried fish for two weeks at best, my lord. Ishtar has kept our stores full until the last season."

Gilgamesh's jaw tightened, and he traced his finger along the map, marking potential weak points in their defenses. "We cannot let it last that long. Perhaps we can force a decisive engagement. But I'd prefer a solution that spares lives. My rash words sparked this, so I must find a way to end it."

A hush settled over the group, each face turned to Gilgamesh in anticipation. They trusted him, despite his long absence and the rumors surrounding his quest for immortality. In their eyes, he saw a reflection of the burden and pride he felt for them. They were his people, and he would stand for them as they had stood by him.

By the time Gilgamesh left the courtyard, night had deepened into a quiet hush. Patrolling guards roamed the walls, their torches flickering against the star-studded sky. He ascended a narrow flight of stairs to a secluded balcony overlooking the city. From this vantage, he saw Uruk's rooftops, the silent tribute to mortal achievement that glimmered faintly beneath the moonlight. He inhaled a deep breath, remembering the illusions he had once held, illusions of a single flower or some grand cosmic secret that could shield him from the pain of mortality.

His grief for Enkidu mixed with a solemn resolve. The truths gleaned from Utnapishtim and the heartbreak of losing the Flower of Renewal had taught him that immortality of the flesh was a hollow pursuit. Instead, he realized, life's meaning came from legacy, the bonds forged in the midst of adversity. If Uruk survived, if he safeguarded its future, that would be immortality enough.

When dawn broke, it revealed the lines of Kish's army starkly drawn against the dusty plains. The day's negotiations had ended in failure, and Gilgamesh steeled himself for war. Yet an idea flickered at the edge of his mind. It was a recollection of ancient times, tales of kings meeting on the battlefield to decide conflict in single combat. Could such a challenge quell the thirst for vengeance on both sides?

His decision made, Gilgamesh donned the armor that had been readied for him, from polished bronze plates, a helm inscribed with the stories of Uruk's might, to the sword that had felled beasts and defied gods. He marched through the city, his presence rekindling hope among his people. Reaching the gates, he signaled for them to open just enough for him to step through. A hush fell on Uruk's defenders; the sight of their king venturing out alone stirred their hearts.

Akka's sentries spotted Gilgamesh's solitary advance, and soon a small crowd of Kish warriors gathered, curiosity piqued. Gilgamesh stopped just beyond bow range, raising his voice in a proclamation that echoed across the field.

"Akka of Kish!" he roared, his tone carrying both pride and

humility. "I stand before you, unarmed except for my sword, to offer single combat. Let our armies watch, and let the matter end with me or you. Spare our people. Let them see that we, as kings, take responsibility for our enmities."

For a moment, there was only stillness. Then a murmur rose among the Kish soldiers, and they parted to reveal Akka himself, striding forward with grim purpose. His armor gleamed in the early light, and the lines of his face were etched with years of bitterness and resolution.

"You would dare suggest single combat after all these years?" Akka's voice thundered, reminiscent of the anger he had nurtured. "Why should I accept?"

"Because I was the one who offended you," Gilgamesh replied, his voice unwavering. "And if you or I should fall, we end this cycle of death before it ravages our cities. I ask you to consider your men, your people, as I consider mine."

A rumble of debate moved through the soldiers of Kish. Akka stood silent, his eyes fixed on Gilgamesh with an unspoken maelstrom of rage. Finally, he gave a single, curt nod. "Very well. I accept, on one condition. Should you lose, Uruk's gates open to my army without resistance. Every treasure, every soul, is mine."

The demand sent a chill through Gilgamesh, but he steeled himself. "And if I win, you withdraw from our walls forever and vow never to threaten Uruk again."

"So be it," Akka said, drawing his sword.

Gilgamesh exhaled, stepping forward, the circle of watching warriors receding to give them space. Uruk's defenders watched from the walls, hearts pounding with a mix of fear and hope. Gilgamesh thought of Enkidu, of the joys they had shared and the lessons learned from Utnapishtim. This was not a fight for mere pride. It was for the people who believed in him, for the city he had built, and for the memory of the friend who had taught him the true worth of life.

He raised his sword, meeting Akka's gaze. The clang of steel against steel rang out, cutting through the hush of dawn. A new chapter began, one where mortal kings clashed to settle an old debt, and where Gilgamesh, having journeyed beyond the reach of mortal understanding, fought to preserve what truly mattered in a fleeting world. "We end this tomorrow at dawn. Go well, and feast your last supper."

Chapter 38:

KILLING FOR FORGIVENESS

The dawn sky cast a muted glow over the plains outside Uruk's mighty walls, the early light transforming the dust and stone into a golden haze. Soldiers from both sides, Kish and Uruk, stood arrayed in watchful silence, forming a vast circle around the two kings who were about to decide the fate of their cities in single combat. From Uruk's walls, hundreds of anxious faces peered out, their eyes fixed on the lone figure of Gilgamesh. He stood at the center of this ring, every inch a king, his polished bronze armor catching the light in brilliant flashes, his sword glinting with the promise of battle. Across from him, King Akka of Kish mirrored his stance, clad in darkened metal plates etched with the scars of past wars, his expression hard and resolute.

A hush weighed on the field, as though even the wind had stilled in deference to the moment. No birds sang, no insects buzzed; there was only the breath of mortal men, and the slow drumbeat of fear and anticipation. Gilgamesh glanced behind him for a final glimpse of Uruk's formidable walls. He felt the gravity of that sight settle into his chest, reminding him that he fought not just for his pride or his life, but for his people, men, women, and children who depended on him to keep them safe.

Akka advanced a step, sword raised in a silent challenge. His gaze pinned Gilgamesh with unspoken anger, the simmering grudge of years past. He was stocky and solid, his powerful frame showing little sign of age, and the lines on his face told the story of a man who had hardened his resolve through many campaigns. His men stood behind him, their voices hushed. Even they seemed uneasy with how personal this battle was, a king's vendetta that had turned into a siege, pitting two once-friendly cities against each other.

Gilgamesh inclined his head in acknowledgment, feeling the warmth of the rising sun on his skin. "This ends today," he said, his voice echoing across the makeshift arena. "For Uruk, for Kish. May only we bear the price of our feud. Let the bloodshed be contained here, between us, and spare our peoples further grief."

Akka's response was a sharp, humorless laugh. "Your concern is too little, too late, Gilgamesh. You speak of sparing grief, but you caused me no small measure of it when you insulted me before my own men. Did you think such a wound would heal on its own?"

Gilgamesh's jaw tightened. He did recall that slight, once a moment's arrogant flourish, which now threatened to tear their lands apart. He forced himself to remain calm. "I was younger then. I see now the cost of pride. If we must fight, then let us fight as kings, not as butchers."

A grim set settled into Akka's features. "Words do not erase dishonor. Draw your sword, Gilgamesh."

Without hesitation, Gilgamesh raised his blade. The polished metal caught the sunlight, throwing a spark into the dawn air. The tension in the circle of warriors reached a breaking point that everyone felt the exact moment when violence became inevitable. Gilgamesh inhaled, remembering Enkidu's face for a heartbeat. Then he charged.

Their swords met with a ring of steel that tore through the silence. Gilgamesh's first strike was swift, angled for Akka's shoulder, testing the reflexes of a foe long overshadowed by memory. Akka parried neatly, redirecting Gilgamesh's blade with a practiced turn of the wrist. A murmur rippled through the gathered men, each one realizing that this was no mere skirmish. This was a clash of seasoned warriors, both driven by cause and consequence.

They traded blows, the sound of steel-on-steel echoing across the field. Gilgamesh fought with precision honed by battles against beasts and gods, his footwork fluid despite the weight of his armor. Akka countered with brutal efficiency, each strike aimed to end the fight swiftly. He fought like a man on a mission, fueled by a wounded pride that demanded Gilgamesh pay in blood.

Dust stirred beneath their feet, swirling around them as they circled and collided. Gilgamesh's breathing grew labored, sweat beading on his brow. The journey he had undertaken had tempered his spirit, but his body bore the fatigue of countless ordeals. Akka, for his part, radiated a grim vigor, his anger lending him vigor that matched Gilgamesh's divine lineage blow for blow.

The watchers held their breath as the kings locked swords, their blades scraping together in a shriek of metal. For a moment, their faces were mere inches apart, each man straining to overpower the other. Gilgamesh's eyes met Akka's, and what he saw there was not just anger, but the hurt of a king who felt his honor trampled by a slight that had festered for too long.

"Why wait so many years?" Gilgamesh hissed between gritted teeth, muscles quivering as he tried to break the stalemate. "We could have settled this when our animosity was young."

Akka pushed back, forcing Gilgamesh to stagger a step. "Because your name grew too great," he spat. "I had to gather an army worthy of challenging you, a legend among men. Even so, I wonder if I can truly best you alone. But I will try."

With a sudden twist, Gilgamesh broke free and lunged, aiming a slash at Akka's midsection. Akka darted aside, barely escaping a crippling blow. The onlookers gasped, the tension so thick it felt like an invisible hand clasping their throats. Gilgamesh pressed his advantage, forcing Akka back with a flurry of strikes that battered his enemy's sword and threatened to slip past his guard. Yet

Akka was no mere novice. He steadied himself and replied with a vicious riposte, nearly catching Gilgamesh's shoulder.

The clash intensified, both kings driving themselves past the limits of endurance. Their swords glinted in the harsh sunlight, arcs of steel weaving a deadly dance. Gilgamesh's armor bore fresh scratches, and blood trickled from a shallow cut on Akka's arm. Each wound, each bruise, further stoked the fires of determination in both men.

Throughout this lethal dance, the armies of Kish and Uruk watched in hushed awe. Soldiers who had stood ready to slay each other now found themselves united in witnessing the skill and ferocity of their respective monarchs. Some from Kish wondered if their lord's thirst for vengeance was justified, seeing Gilgamesh's prowess overshadow their preconceptions. Meanwhile, Uruk's defenders found their hope rekindled at the sight of Gilgamesh, returned from an otherworldly journey, standing firm to protect them yet again.

Time became unmoored, the battle stretching into a blur of lunges and parries, of gasping breaths and thunderous heartbeats. Sweat poured from Gilgamesh's brow, and with each passing minute, he felt the weight of his exhaustion. Yet he also felt a strange sense of clarity. The ephemeral nature of mortal life, the burdens of pride and regret, the lessons of Utnapishtim, Siduri, and his own heartbreak, these all formed a tapestry that reminded him why he fought. He fought to preserve life's fragile beauty, not to revel in dominance or subjugation.

Finally, a misstep from Akka opened an opportunity. Gilgamesh seized it with lightning reflexes, sidestepping a hasty thrust. He slammed his sword against Akka's guard, knocking the blade from his rival's hand. In the same fluid motion, he swiveled and brought his sword hilt crashing into Akka's helmet with a dull thud. The King of Kish staggered, dazed, and fell heavily to one knee. His sword clattered on the ground a pace away, unreachable.

The hush over the battlefield deepened, every eye fixed on the outcome. Gilgamesh, breathing hard, stood over Akka, sword raised, poised to deliver the final strike. Time itself seemed to slow, the wind holding its breath. A single thrust, and Gilgamesh's victory would be complete. He saw in Akka's eyes a blend of resignation and anger, the acceptance of a man who had gambled everything on a final confrontation.

Gilgamesh hesitated, the lines of his face contorting with emotion. He thought of how easily a life could be snuffed out, how death had claimed Enkidu. He remembered the goddess Ishtar's wrath, the cruelty of fate, and the fleeting wonder of every breath. If he struck now, vengeance would be satisfied, but he would be perpetuating the cycle of violence that had brought Kish's army to his doorstep. The world did not need another testament to the ruthlessness of kings; it needed an end to pride's vicious circle.

He lowered his sword, voice raw but resolute. "I will not kill you, Akka."

A tremor of disbelief rippled through the watching armies. Kish's soldiers tensed, wondering if this was a trick, while Uruk's defenders looked on with a mixture of relief and awe. Gilgamesh knelt, his blade laid flat on the ground. Reaching out, he grasped Akka's shoulder gently, meeting his gaze.

"You have your honor," Gilgamesh said. "You stood against me, fought bravely. And I have no wish to see more blood spilled on account of a long-ago insult. Take your army and go. Return to Kish. Let your wrath end here, so our people may live in peace."

Akka blinked, the sting of defeat evident in his eyes. Sweat and blood trickled down his brow. He swallowed hard, his lips parting as though to speak, but no words emerged. The anger and bitterness that had fueled him for so long seemed to war with a dawning realization. He had been beaten, and yet spared. Slowly, he bowed his head, a tremor running through him as if something within had finally cracked.

"You… would let me live?" he asked at last, his voice rasping with fatigue.

Gilgamesh nodded, rising to his feet. He offered Akka a hand. "I have seen enough death for one lifetime, Akka. My quest for immortality showed me the emptiness of vengeance. Accept this mercy, and let us not condemn thousands more to die for our pride."

For a heartbeat, the two men remained locked in a silent exchange. Then, with a halting motion, Akka clasped Gilgamesh's hand and stood, his legs unsteady. He glanced around, meeting the eyes of his closest soldiers, who looked on with shock and tentative relief. The King of Kish sighed, rubbing the bruise on his temple, wrestling inwardly with the aftermath of his defeat.

"Very well," he said, voice subdued. "I will take my men and leave your lands. This debt ends here." He swallowed again, as though the words themselves were bitter. "I… thank you, Gilgamesh, for your mercy. You have shown yourself the greater man."

A wave of disbelief and cautious hope rippled through both armies. Slowly, the circle of warriors broke, men from Kish moving toward their king, men from Uruk rushing to Gilgamesh's side. Some from Kish looked as though they could not decide whether to be relieved or outraged that they would leave without pillaging the city. But the moment of bloodshed had passed, and it seemed none were eager to contest the kings' pact.

Gilgamesh turned to his own soldiers, relief flooding his expression. Many clasped his arm, their voices low with gratitude. The weight of responsibility he carried felt lighter, knowing he had averted disaster not through conquest but through restraint. In that moment, the lessons of his long journey, from Siduri's compassion, Utnapishtim's sorrow, to the fleeting wonder of life, all coalesced into a newfound perspective on leadership and destiny.

Drums began to sound, signaling the retreat of Kish's forces. The tents that ringed Uruk were taken down, the enemy's camp dissipating like a mirage. Soldiers from both cities watched each other warily, but slowly, the hostility faded as ranks thinned and the demand for retribution waned. Gilgamesh stood on a small rise near the city walls, observing the exodus. The dust of their departure rose into the air like a benediction of peace, though his heart still hammered with the adrenaline of the fight.

Akka approached him again, his posture rigid but respectful. "We will go now. I leave with my pride wounded, but not shattered. Know this, Gilgamesh, I do not forget a debt of mercy. Should you ever need aid, send word, and perhaps our peoples can forge bonds instead of hostilities."

Gilgamesh inclined his head, an unexpected warmth in his chest at the offer. "I welcome such a day, King Akka. Let us part as men who understand the cost of war and the value of peace."

They clasped forearms, a gesture of solidarity that echoed across the battlefield. Then Akka mounted his horse, his retainers forming around him, and they departed, the long columns of Kish's soldiers trailing behind them like a serpent relinquishing its prey. Gilgamesh watched until they vanished into the distance, the tension in his muscles ebbing away as the threat receded.

Exhausted but triumphant, he returned to Uruk's gates. The people lined the streets, cheering as he passed, their relief evident in their tear-streaked faces. Gilgamesh felt a pang of emotion at their adulation. He had sought immortality, yet found himself cherishing their mortal lives more deeply than ever.

In the palace courtyard, Gilgamesh stripped off his battered armor, the weight of it feeling heavier now that the danger had passed. A hush enveloped the courtyard as citizens and warriors alike gathered around him. Arumak, the trusted soldier, stepped forward, his gaze bright with admiration and something like reverence.

"You have saved us, my king," Arumak said, kneeling. "Uruk stands unbroken."

Gilgamesh lifted him by the shoulders. "Rise, friend. We have all done our part. This victory belongs to Uruk, not just to me."

A roar of approval rose from the gathered crowd, a sound of relief and unity that echoed through the city's mighty walls. In that moment, Gilgamesh saw the legacy he had nearly abandoned in pursuit of a flower that promised eternal youth. This community of beating hearts was the immortality worth cherishing.

Night fell over Uruk, but the city did not sleep. Fires burned in the streets, torches lit the walls, and families emerged from their bolted doors to celebrate. Laughter and song replaced fear's tight grip. Gilgamesh found himself in the palace's great hall, surrounded by jubilant faces. Yet in the midst of the revelry, he slipped away to a small balcony overlooking the city.

He gazed at the lights dancing across Uruk's rooftops. The hum of life and love, of fellowship and bonds forged in shared trials, moved him more deeply than any cosmic revelation had. He recalled the serpent that stole his hard-won flower, the brutal confrontation he'd survived, and the mercy he had chosen to show King Akka. Each experience was a thread in the tapestry of his growth, a tapestry woven not by the gods, but by his mortal choices.

From the darkness behind him, a familiar voice spoke softly. "You have fought many battles, Gilgamesh," it said, though no one was there to hear it. "Yet the greatest battle was the one you waged with yourself. In mercy, you found a spark of that eternal truth you sought."

He did not turn, nor did he search for the source of those words. Whether they were memories of Siduri's counsel, an echo of Enkidu's bond, or the whisper of his own conscience, he accepted them as the silent wisdom that guided him now. He closed his eyes, breathing in the night air that carried the smell of cooking fires and desert wind. This was life. It was fleeting, precious, and immeasurably profound.

He leaned against the balcony rail, a wry smile curving his lips as he stared into the stars. The countless pinpricks of light reminded him of the wonders he had seen, the illusions he had chased. Perhaps tomorrow would bring new challenges or new sorrows. But tonight, he would allow himself the comfort of knowing that Uruk was safe, that his people could rest without fear.

As the torches burned down and songs finally quieted, Gilgamesh remained on the balcony, watching the sky shift from twilight's purple to the velvet of true night. Enkidu's memory warmed his chest like a gentle ember, a reminder that mortality, though finite, was a vessel for the greatest treasures of all. They were friendship, honor, and compassion. The epic of his life continued, and though he could not escape the fate of all men, he had learned to face it with a heart unbowed.

Tomorrow, he would lead Uruk in rebuilding its defenses, in forging new ties that might one day bridge the gap between kingdoms. But for now, he let the peace settle over him, content in the knowledge that for this night, at least, he had saved his people and chosen mercy over revenge. In that mercy lay the true immortality he had sought, a living testament to the power of mortal hearts to shape the world, even in the shadow of gods and the specter of death.

Chapter 39

A LOOK AT WHAT IS TO COME

Gilgamesh slept in the hush of the late night, the distant lights of Uruk's torches flickering beyond his windows. His mind, weary from the turmoil of battle and the heaviness of life's revelations, drifted into a realm of visions. At first, the dream enveloped him in a gentle warmth, like soft clouds gathering around a sunset sky. Yet, just as quickly, it shifted, and he found himself in a vast, unknown land, standing among towering structures that seemed both miraculous and confounding to his eyes.

He beheld a great tower reaching far above him, its top vanishing into the sky. The structure was of a design he could not comprehend, made of bricks that shone strangely in the dream's bright haze. People thronged around it, speaking in a cacophony of tongues. The sound of it battered Gilgamesh's ears, reminiscent of the confusion of city markets but magnified a hundredfold. He saw men and women toiling, carrying bricks and mortar, building and building without end, as though they sought to pierce the very dome of the heavens. A nervous feeling tugged at him. This tower was reminiscent of an attempt to breach the gods' domain, a challenge not unlike his own ambition. Yet something about it felt doomed, as though pride spurred them onward to a cosmic folly.

As he tried to approach, the dream warped, pulling him away like a gust of wind snatching a leaf. The tower and its crowds vanished in a swirl of color and sound. His vision blurred, and he found himself standing in a vast, arid countryside. The sky was harshly bright, the land dotted with scraggly shrubs and a scattering of houses crafted from baked clay. There was a hush, heavy and foreboding, and far ahead, he saw a crowd gathered around a wooden structure. The shapes of men and women, robed in garments foreign to him, pressed together, their voices subdued. A figure was raised upon beams of wood, arms outstretched, a crown of thorns upon his head. Gilgamesh recognized the expression on the figure's face as one of profound sorrow and love, though it was a love he could not fully understand. The figure's blood dripped onto the ground, the crowd either jeering or weeping.

Gilgamesh's heart lurched at the sight. The man on the cross exuded a transcendent aura, unlike any mortal he had known. It reminded him of the presence he felt in the Garden of the Gods, a sense of universal significance that transcended words. Yet the scene was filled with cruel suffering, and Gilgamesh could not fathom why a being so radiant was met with nails and agony. He reached out, wanting to intervene, to fight the injustice as he would fight any beast or tyrant. But the dream would not allow it. His limbs felt weighed by invisible chains. He called out, voice echoing in a voiceless realm, but no one heard him.

The vision shifted again, as though time itself fractured and rearranged. This time, he was surrounded by darkness punctuated by small pockets of feeble light, a dim era of confusion. The land seemed drained of color, the people huddled in cloaks of rough wool, fear etched into their faces. Stones that once formed towering buildings were scattered as rubble, and knowledge was hoarded in cramped places, revered but hidden. Gilgamesh walked through desolate villages where life was meager, as though a shadow had fallen upon the world. It felt to him like a dark age indeed, a time when learning and wonder had retreated behind fortress walls. He saw flickers of conflict, of men in crude iron armor clashing, not for glory or even survival, but for scraps of power. A deep sadness swelled within him, recalling his battles that had at least carried a sense of purpose. Here, it seemed, war was an endless cycle of bleakness. He wanted to cry out to them, to remind them of the fleeting wonder of life, but they seemed deaf to his presence.

That world dissolved into swirling sparks of color. An eerie stillness filled his dream, broken by an incomprehensible roar that shook the very fabric of the vision. He found himself in a vast city of gleaming towers, impossibly tall, made of metal and glass. Strange wheeled machines roared through the streets, and the air hummed with an unearthly energy. Gilgamesh struggled to grasp these wonders. This was a civilization so far removed from his time that it felt like the realm of gods. People wore garments of colors and cuts he had never seen, moving with a frantic, purposeful stride. He tried to speak to them, but once again, he was invisible, a silent observer to a future that defied understanding.

Then, with a sudden jolt, the city melted into a shrieking wind of light. There was an immense flash, a piercing brightness that burned everything in its path. Gilgamesh's eyes widened, the radiance a thousand times the glare of the desert sun. A silent explosion expanded in a great, roiling cloud, blooming like a sinister mushroom that blotted the sky. The force of it ripped through concrete and steel, leveling the city in a heartbeat. Gilgamesh felt a terror that dwarfed any he had known, a primal recognition that this was destruction on a scale beyond the gods' anger. No storm or flood he had heard of could rival this man-made cataclysm. He wanted to scream, to curse the folly that had given mortals the power to annihilate themselves so utterly.

The afterimage seared into his vision, leaving him blinking in darkness. An unholy quiet followed, as if the entire dream paused to let the weight of this devastation settle into his soul. He felt a deep tremor of sorrow for the people of that time, for their achievements undone by a single, blinding moment. A wave of sympathy and horror coursed through him, reminiscent of the pity he felt for those lost in the great flood, but amplified by knowledge that man, not the gods, had wrought this end.

Overcome, he tried to flee, but the dream would not release

him. The darkness pulsed, giving way to a faint, shimmering glow. Within that glow, a figure manifested who was tall, muscular, hair wild as a lion's mane. Gilgamesh's heart lifted. It was Enkidu, the soul who had walked beside him in both joy and tragedy. Enkidu stood with open arms, eyes shining with warmth and love. A radiant light enveloped him, and Gilgamesh felt tears burn his cheeks. The dear companion he had lost was here, luminous and welcoming.

He reached out, a strangled cry escaping his lips. "Enkidu…"

The name tasted of ashes and memories, of laughter and tears. Enkidu did not speak, but his expression bore all the words Gilgamesh needed. The brilliant light grew, enveloping Gilgamesh in its radiance. He felt the burdens of his journey lift, if only for a heartbeat. In that indescribable brightness, Gilgamesh sensed a profound serenity, a reflection of the intangible truth that love might stretch beyond mortal constraints, bridging the chasm between life and death.

He tried to move closer, but an unseen force restrained him, as though the dream existed behind a thin but unbreakable barrier. Enkidu's eyes, full of compassion, seemed to speak. They said, "There is a boundary even you cannot cross in life. Not yet." The paradox of it seared Gilgamesh's soul, torn between the longing to be reunited and the duty calling him back to wakefulness.

Tears slipped from his cheeks as his friend's image began to fade. Gilgamesh fought against it, straining to remain in that golden realm. He wanted to cling to Enkidu's presence, to beg for answers, to promise that he would make good on all they had dreamed. But the dream's final threads unraveled, pulling him into a swirl of color and emotion that dissolved into the star-dappled darkness of sleep.

He awoke to the faint light of predawn in Uruk, the dull ache of reality settling into his bones. The echoes of that cataclysmic vision churned in his mind like fragments from a broken cosmic tapestry. He did not comprehend the symbols or the epoch-spanning story they told, only that they were glimpses of events far beyond his life's small window.

In that half-awake state, Gilgamesh reflected on the strange continuity of humankind's potential for creation and destruction, love and madness. He thought of the tower that soared to the heavens, undone by pride. He saw the crucified figure, a sorrowful testament to sacrifice, and an age of darkness where knowledge lay in fragile pockets of hope. And then the final horror, that luminous wave of annihilation wrought not by the gods, but by mortal hands.

A tremor of realization coursed through him, that mankind, across all ages, wrestled with forces that mirrored the gods in both creative and destructive power. The impetus behind building a tower to the sky or forging a bomb that could tear cities apart shared a root in ambition and fear. And each time, a tragedy or a lesson arose, perhaps too late, to humble those who overreached.

Yet, in the glow of his dream's last fleeting vision, Enkidu had stood, arms extended in a silent embrace, as though to say that love and memory could endure even when the world itself faltered. For Gilgamesh, it was a comforting sign that his brother's spirit remained near, a guiding star in the vast unknown.

He pushed himself to a seated position on his bed, the night's chill air prickling his skin. Outside, the hush of Uruk lay over the city, broken by the faint stirring of early vendors setting up their stalls. He realized that in all the future horrors he had witnessed, mankind still persisted. Humanity still built, prayed, and wept. For Gilgamesh, that fragile persistence became a source of hope. If, in the far future, man could endure such cataclysms, maybe his own city could also find the resilience to flourish in the shadow of mortal strife.

His mind drifted to the siege he had recently broken, the final confrontation with King Akka that ended in mercy rather than further bloodshed. He had come close to repeating the same cycle of vengeance that brought destruction to so many across the ages. Yet, he chose mercy. Was that choice not an echo of the sacrifice and love glimpsed in his dream? He believed so. Perhaps in forging a world guided by empathy and wisdom, he was forging a new path that might spare his people from the dooms he had foreseen.

As the first hints of dawn streaked the sky with pale color, Gilgamesh rose, slipping from his chamber and onto a small balcony that overlooked Uruk's broad streets. In the distance, the great walls stood as silent guardians, gilded by the faintest glimmer of morning. The city, though battered by siege and haunted by fear, began to stir with life once more. Merchants readied their wares, farmers led livestock from cramped stalls, and children peered cautiously from doorways, as though testing the day for threats.

Gilgamesh exhaled a deep breath, letting the crisp air fill his lungs. He thought of all he had witnessed in that dream. Though he grasped only fragments of meaning, one thing stood clear, and that was humanity's capacity for both creation and destruction transcended even the boundaries of time. The illusions of immortality or indefinite power led to heartbreak or chaos, unless tempered by love and compassion.

He placed a hand gently on his chest, recalling the silent presence of Enkidu in the final moment of the dream. The memory felt like a warm glow, an assurance that life's true immortality sprang from bonds of friendship and the legacies they forged. If the ages ahead were to be believed, mankind would ascend to glorious heights and sink to dreadful lows. But they would also endure, guided by the spark of hope that he could now carry back to his own people.

In that quiet moment, Gilgamesh made a silent vow to honor what he had gleaned from his night's turbulent visions. He would guard Uruk, love his people, and cherish each dawn. He would remember that the greatest gift was life's fragility, its fleeting nature urging them to strive for wisdom and kindness. And one day, when his mortal breath ceased, he would meet Enkidu again in that realm of bright light, arms wide in a welcome that transcended even the gods' design.

Chapter 40:

GUIDANCE OF TWO GODS

The palace halls of Uruk were quiet in the early morning light. The corridors, usually alive with the murmurs of servants and the shuffle of petitioners, lay hushed, bathed in the gentle glow of dawn. Gilgamesh wandered those passages alone, each footfall echoing against the polished stone floors. His thoughts hung heavy on him. He had memories of the siege, the serpent that stole his hard-won Flower of Renewal, and the haunting visions of civilizations far beyond his comprehension. All these weighed upon the mortal king who had touched the edges of the divine.

He made his way toward the temple of his mother, Ninsun, guided by the warmth of torches flickering in ornate wall sconces. That ancient comfort drew him forward. If there was any one mortal or immortal who could soothe his troubled mind, it was she. Ninsun, a goddess in her own right, had the wisdom of heaven and the compassion of a mother's love. Gilgamesh paused outside her temple, steeling himself for the flood of questions he would bring and the truths he might receive.

He stepped inside. Ninsun sat by a low table, steam rising from a bowl of herbs. She looked up, her eyes filled with immediate understanding. Without a word, she beckoned him closer. Gilgamesh approached, bowing his head in greeting.

"Mother," he said, voice hushed. "I have returned."

201

Ninsun stood and placed a hand against his cheek, her gaze traveling over the lines of sorrow etched into her son's face. "I know," she said softly, guiding him to a cushioned seat. "I could sense your trials, as though the heavens carried whispers of your path. You have walked in dark places, Gilgamesh."

He closed his eyes momentarily, remembering the cold depths of the Water of Death, the echoing hush of the Garden of the Gods, and the serpent's theft of his last hope of immortality. "I sought so much," he confessed. "I sought to defy death and bring back what was taken from me. Yet every path I have walked has brought new burdens."

Ninsun poured a fragrant tea into a clay cup and passed it to him. "Tell me all you have seen."

So he recounted his journey. Ninsun listened with grave attention, her fingers tapping absently at the table's worn surface. When he finished, she sighed, a sound laced with both empathy and resignation.

"You traveled beyond mortal boundaries, my child. You witnessed wonders and terrors," she said. "These trials were not yours alone to bear. My heart grieved with each step you took into the unknown. But you must understand, Gilgamesh, that even the gods cannot undo what is ordained in the deep currents of fate."

Gilgamesh's jaw tightened. "Are we then slaves to destiny? Must I simply accept the gods' whims, as though my free will matters for nothing?"

She stroked his hair gently, in a gesture that reminded him of simpler times. "We all play our parts in the grand tapestry, whether god or mortal. The difference lies in how we embrace what is given. You have defied the gods, yes, but always from a place of love and need. And still, their decrees hold. They will not last forever, Gilgamesh. Even they must bend to forces greater than themselves, in the far future where time unravels. But until that distant day, we must accept what they bring to us."

He bowed his head, wrestling with her words. "I have seen in dreams a world beyond even the gods' grasp, a place where man unleashes destruction upon itself. Could it be that time outlives the gods?"

She closed her eyes, sadness in her expression. "In some future age, the gods may fade, their names forgotten by mortals who find new powers to worship or to wield. But that day is not yet. You remain in an age where they still reign, and the consequences of defying them can be dire. You stand on the cusp, living with a foot in two worlds, the mortal realm you cherish and the cosmic realm that holds power over you."

Gilgamesh's hands clenched around the clay cup. "Then how am I to live, knowing that death is inevitable, that Enkidu's fate awaits us all, yet that I have glimpsed truths beyond mortal reach? What solace is there, Mother?"

Ninsun's gaze softened. "Solace rests in the life you choose to lead. You have witnessed how mercy can conquer pride. You have learned that bonds of love, forged in mortal hearts, can outlast even the mightiest walls. Your immortality lies not in a cosmic boon, but in how you shape the days granted to you and how your people will remember you."

He exhaled a long breath, a gentle ache in his chest. "I hear you," he said. "Though my heart still yearns for answers."

She rested her hand on his shoulder. "Answers come, but in their own time."

A knock at the door broke their quiet exchange. A soldier, helm tucked under his arm, entered and bowed deeply. "My king," he addressed Gilgamesh, voice quivering with subdued excitement. "Shamash has come. He stands in the courtyard, asking for you."

Gilgamesh's brow rose. It was not unusual for Shamash to appear as he had guided Gilgamesh on past journeys, but rarely did the sun god walk the mortal halls so openly. Ninsun gave a faint nod, a flicker of understanding passing between them. Together, they rose and followed the soldier through winding corridors.

They emerged into the palace courtyard to find Shamash standing by a mosaic fountain. The god's radiance was tempered into mortal form, but his presence still dazzled. Clad in robes that shimmered with the hues of dawn, he cast an aura of calm authority. Attendants drew back, heads bowed, unsure how to approach one who straddled the divine and mortal realms so casually.

"Gilgamesh," Shamash called, his voice imbued with celestial warmth. "I have come to speak with you."

Gilgamesh inclined his head respectfully. "Shamash," he replied. "You honor us with your presence."

Shamash moved closer, his amber eyes reflecting empathy. "You have journeyed far, beyond the boundaries of life and death. I have watched, lending what aid I could, but I see the sorrow in your eyes. Your path has taken its toll."

Gilgamesh looked down. "I sought immortality, yet found only fleeting glimpses of truth. I forced a siege to end by my own strength and mercy, but the scars remain. I stand here, no closer to transcending fate than any man."

Shamash lifted his gaze to the horizon, where the spires of Uruk glimmered under the sun's first rays. "Fate binds mortals and gods alike, Gilgamesh. You cling to the hope of conquering death, but consider the joys that arise from mortality. It is life's brevity that makes each moment precious. Would you strip your people of that wonder?"

Gilgamesh's throat tightened. He thought of Enkidu's laughter, the ephemeral joy of festivals in Uruk, the love that flourished in each fleeting season. "I do not wish to strip away their wonder," he said quietly. "I only sought to preserve it, to spare them the pain of loss."

A gentle smile touched Shamash's lips. "And yet, loss

carves a space for love to take deeper root. Without endings, would beginnings hold any magic? Even we gods, for all our might, will one day face our dusk. Time outlives even the divine, in ages too distant for mortal eyes."

Gilgamesh remembered the visions in his dream. A thread of realization tugged at him. First, that Shamash and Ninsun must have noticed his thoughts. Second, that even the gods were not eternal in the grand cosmic scheme. He studied Shamash, seeking confirmation in the sun god's timeless gaze.

Shamash nodded, as though hearing Gilgamesh's silent thoughts. "That distant day will come, though it lies beyond our horizon. We gods hold dominion now, but we do not deny our eventual end. It is the law of the cosmos."

Ninsun stepped forward, placing a reassuring hand on Gilgamesh's arm. "Do you see now, my son? Though the gods hold sway, their reign is not without limits. They, too, are bound. And so, we mortals and immortals alike must accept what we cannot change, and discover meaning in the life we have."

Gilgamesh let out a slow breath, the tension in his shoulders easing. "I think I begin to understand. The gods will do as they do until their time is ended. We mortals must live under that shadow, yet still find our own light."

Shamash's smile widened, radiating genuine warmth. "Well spoken, Gilgamesh. You have learned that immortality is no treasure to hold in your hand, but a seed to plant in your deeds, your love, and the memory that lingers when you are gone. Your journey has tested you in ways few could endure, and you have emerged stronger, if not invincible."

Gilgamesh dipped his head in gratitude. "Thank you, Shamash, for guiding me when I needed it, for urging me to reflect when all I saw was rage. I owe you a debt I cannot repay."

A mild chuckle escaped Shamash. "Your growth is repayment

enough. I delight to see a king who treads with both strength and compassion. Continue as you have, Gilgamesh. Protect Uruk, love your people, and hold close to the bonds that define you."

Ninsun turned to her son, her gaze brimming with affection. "My child, you have stood against man, beast, and god. You have seen that pride alone wins nothing, and that mercy can save many. In your mortal days, live well, and let the glory of your name be forged by love rather than fear."

Gilgamesh bowed, emotions stirring deep within him. He recalled the fierce heat of his early reign, the brash arrogance that once led him to dismiss mortal life as trifling. Now, after so many trials, he felt the fragile grace of each breath. "Mother," he said, voice almost trembling, "I will not waste this understanding. I will rule Uruk with a gentle hand and an unyielding spirit, if the gods permit me the years to do so."

Shamash's form shimmered slightly, a subtle reminder of his divine nature. "Your path continues, Gilgamesh. Though your quest for an artifact of immortality was in vain, you have grasped something far more profound. Remember it when doubt returns, as it will. Live fully. Defy cruelty. Embrace love."

With that, the sun god inclined his head. A breeze stirred the courtyard, and the torch flames flickered. Gilgamesh blinked, and in that instant, Shamash was gone, his essence dissolved into the sunlight that bathed the palace. The faint echo of his laughter lingered, like the final chord of a distant melody.

Ninsun released a soft breath, her eyes bright with a mother's pride. "He is right, you know," she said. "Doubt will come. You will face it time and again. But the answers lie not in defying the gods, nor in clinging to illusions of eternal life. They lie in the very world before you. It is in your city, your people, and the connections you forge."

Gilgamesh turned from the spot where Shamash had stood, meeting his mother's gaze. Her strength and compassion warmed him, reminiscent of the love he had found in Enkidu's friendship. "I accept the fate they bring," he said slowly. "Though it grieves me that the world must lose so much to time, I choose to cherish what remains."

Ninsun's hand found his, giving it a gentle squeeze. "You have grown in wisdom, my son. That, in itself, is a kind of immortality."

Together, they left the courtyard. Sunlight spilled through the palace windows, greeting them with each step as if to welcome Gilgamesh's return to the mortal realm. The corridors were no longer silent. The servants bustled about, preparing for the day. The hush of curiosity followed the king wherever he went. Word of his meeting with Shamash already spread, mingling awe with excitement.

As Gilgamesh made his way toward the throne room, he pondered the significance of the old gods. Yes, they still reigned, their power shaping the world. But he had glimpsed a future in his dreams, a future where mortal ambition scaled heights unknown and wrought horrors beyond imagination. He had heard from his mother and from Shamash that even the gods themselves would one day fade. That was too vast a notion for him to fully comprehend, but he accepted the paradox. The gods would endure until their end came, and mortals must live under that dominion, yet find strength in doing so.

Outside the palace gates, Uruk's streets were waking to life. Merchants opened their stalls, the scent of spiced bread and roasting meats drifting in the air. Children laughed, playing in the dusty squares, their eyes bright with wonder. Warriors returned from their watch, the clank of armor weaving a reassuring note in the city's morning song. Gilgamesh moved among them, acknowledging their greetings with a soft smile. He felt their love more keenly now, an ever-present reminder that though his life was finite, his deeds could bind them all.

A soft breeze rustled through the city, carrying with it the whispers of gods and mortals alike. Gilgamesh found himself gazing skyward, the ephemeral clouds drifting across a tender blue. Perhaps, in ages beyond these days, man would rise to challenge fate in ways unimaginable. Perhaps, too, new pantheons would be born or dethroned, their stories bleeding into the tapestry of time. The future was a mystery, but the present was his to shape.

As the sun climbed higher, he inhaled the scents of his city. He sensed sweat and spice, laughter and resolve, dust and dreams. This was his realm, his destiny. The gods might decree his mortal boundaries, but he wielded the power to fill each hour with meaning. One day he would die, a mortal undone by mortal constraints. Yet he would not die without carving his story into the hearts of his people, ensuring that love and memory could outlast the ephemeral bloom of his breath.

Gilgamesh's mother, Ninsun, soon parted from his side, leaving him to attend to his duties. He entered the throne room, the high ceilings echoing with the soft tread of his sandals. There, scribes awaited with tablets of city affairs, captains with reports of watchful borders, and petitioners needing judgments. Gilgamesh took his seat on the throne, feeling the gravity of rulership settle on his shoulders. But now, that weight no longer felt like a cage. It felt like the promise of life itself. It was fleeting, precious, and an honor to uphold.

In that moment, he recalled Shamash's parting words, "Live fully. Defy cruelty. Embrace love." A faint, determined smile curved his lips. He would do so. For all the trials he had weathered and the illusions he had lost, Gilgamesh still stood. He would guard Uruk, cherish his people, and accept the shifting tapestry of existence. It held Gods above, mortals below, and a destiny he would shape in the space between.

Chapter 41

THE EPIC OF GILGAMESH

Gilgamesh stood upon the walls of Uruk in the fading light of sunset, leaning on a staff fashioned from ancient cedar. Once, he had leapt atop these battlements with a vigor born of youth and divine blood. Now, at the dusk of his reign, the king's broad shoulders and muscled arms bore the softened contours of age. His hair, once a thick mane, had thinned and become a web of silver, and the lines on his face testified to countless wars, adventures, and burdens faced. Yet there remained in his eyes a spark, an inner flame that refused to die. It was the spirit that had once carried him beyond mortal boundaries, seeking the secret of eternity.

The sky glowed with fiery orange and gold, and the great city of Uruk sprawled below him, her walls still proudly upright, her streets alive with the hum of daily life. Gilgamesh's gaze swept over the city he had built and defended, recalling how he had once stood here in the arrogance of youth, certain that his might would forever surpass the grasp of mortality. Now, the old king felt peace settle in his bones, acceptance grown from the memory of so many trials.

He bowed his head, remembering the final hours he had spent with his dear friend Enkidu, stolen by death. He recalled his fruitless chase for the Flower of Renewal, devoured by a cunning serpent. He thought of the countless lessons gleaned from Siduri and Utnapishtim, both immortals, each bearing the lonely burden of outliving mortal loves. All these recollections rose like gentle phantoms, lingering at the edges of his thoughts.

Behind him, the hush of footsteps announced the arrival of a small group of attendants. Gilgamesh turned slowly to greet them. Once, his step would have been agile, but now he moved with careful deliberation, reliant on his staff. The attendants bowed. At their head was Arumak, the warrior-turned-councilor who had once led Gilgamesh's soldiers under siege. Age, too, had left lines upon Arumak's face, yet his voice remained steady, filled with reverence.

"My king," Arumak said, his tone formal but affectionate. "It is growing late. Will you not come down from the walls to rest?"

Gilgamesh offered a soft smile, glancing again at the crimson horizon. "I will," he replied, his voice mild, like a distant echo of thunder now subdued. "I only needed a moment to look upon Uruk, to remember how far we have come."

Arumak stepped closer, gaze flicking with concern over the king's pale features. "The city stands strong," he murmured. "Just as you built her to be. You can rest, knowing your legacy endures."

Gilgamesh inclined his head, acknowledging Arumak's reassurance. "Yes," he said, voice thick with emotion. "My people are my legacy. Their love, their hope… that is the immortality that I once sought so fiercely in distant lands."

He turned and walked toward the steps descending into the city, each step carefully placed. Arumak remained close, ready to steady him if he faltered. Their journey through the streets was a quiet one, the citizens recognizing their king's condition and giving him space. Some bowed in respect, a few whispered thanks for the walls that had repelled enemies and the roads that had brought prosperity. Others remembered stories of Gilgamesh's feats told over glowing hearths.

By the time Gilgamesh reached the palace courtyard, the last brilliance of the sunset had fled the sky. Torches flickered around the polished stone columns, illuminating the scene with a golden glow. An old excitement sprang to life in Gilgamesh's chest, reminding him of the grand feasts and ceremonies that had once filled these halls with song and merriment. Yet now, the hall was largely quiet. Servants scurried about, mindful of the hush that befitted the king's ailing condition.

He continued through the corridors, each footstep a gentle echo. His chamber, near the heart of the palace, welcomed him with the soft glow of a single lamp. Inside, plush cushions and fine tapestries told of a king's grandeur, but Gilgamesh ignored such trappings. He settled onto a long couch, thankful for its comfort. Arumak helped him remove his worn sandals and cloak, carefully placing his staff aside.

"Thank you, friend," Gilgamesh said quietly. "The day has been long. I will rest now."

Arumak bowed. "I shall be just nearby, sire," he said. "Should you need anything."

Left alone, Gilgamesh exhaled slowly, letting his gaze sweep the chamber. On a low table rested mementos of his reign. There was an ornate sword he once wielded in battle and a small carving of Enkidu kneeling beside a lion. He thought of the old days, and his heart ached with a bittersweet longing. For all the trials he had faced, he had come to cherish the fleeting brightness of mortal life over any illusions of eternal vigor.

Exhaustion weighed on him, and he lay back, allowing his eyes to close. Though his body was frail with age, his mind wandered through the corridors of memory, guided by the gentle lull of half-sleep. Outside, the occasional footstep of a guard or servant broke the hush, but inside his mind, the thrumming of years past took shape as vivid recollections.

In that haze of memory, he saw Enkidu once more. There they raced each other through the fields beyond Uruk, dust swirling at their heels, laughter rising like a shared anthem. The old sorrow welled in Gilgamesh's chest but no longer felt so sharp. It was a soft ache, like an ancient melody that lingered in his soul.

He drifted further into slumber. Somewhere in the distance, the old palace dog barked softly, and the night's wind whispered against the windows.

All at once, a dream crept upon him. He found himself on the walls again, yet the city was different. It was brighter, more serene. The walls were bathed in a warm, perpetual glow. He looked up, expecting to see the looming weight of the night sky, but instead the heavens were open and shimmering, like a tapestry of swirling lights. A presence stood beside him. It was his mother, Ninsun, clad in robes that radiated gentle starlight.

"You have walked a long path, my son," she spoke in a voice that reverberated with love.

Gilgamesh turned to her, feeling tears threaten to spill. "Yes," he whispered. "And still I yearn for one last glimpse of the friend I lost."

Ninsun's gaze flicked past him, and Gilgamesh followed it. Standing at the edge of the wall was Enkidu, looking just as he had in life. He was strong-limbed and eyes alight with wild devotion. Gilgamesh's heart clenched, and he tried to step forward, but a wave of dizziness overtook him. In the dream, he staggered, the illusions swirling around him. Yet Enkidu held out his arms in welcome, that old, fierce grin shining on his face.

"Come, Gilgamesh," Enkidu seemed to say, though his lips did not move. "We have so much to share."

Gilgamesh's dream self mustered the last of his strength, reaching toward that radiant figure. The warmth of Enkidu's presence washed over him like a benediction of acceptance. There was no condemnation, no regrets, only an abiding love that transcended years and realms. Gilgamesh felt something inside him unraveling, a lifetime's tension dissolving into peace.

Back in the waking world, a faint tremor ran through his body. His breaths grew shallow, lips parted as he murmured words too soft for any ear to catch. A subtle hush descended upon the chamber, a hush more profound than the quiet of night. This was a hush that signaled a crossing between worlds.

Outside his room, Arumak paced, some primal instinct prompting him to check on the king. He stepped in and found Gilgamesh lying on his couch, eyes closed, features serene. The old warrior froze, a cold prickle traveling down his spine. Quietly, he knelt at the king's side, placing a trembling hand against Gilgamesh's shoulder.

"Sire?" he whispered.

Gilgamesh did not stir. His chest, once so broad and strong, remained still. The faint lines of pain that had furrowed his brow in recent weeks were smoothed away, replaced by a gentle calm. Arumak swallowed thickly, tears brimming in his eyes as he realized that Gilgamesh, King of Uruk, child of the gods, had breathed his last mortal breath.

A soft cry escaped Arumak's lips, echoing through the empty corridors. Guards and attendants rushed in, confusion and grief etched upon their faces. One by one, they understood what had happened, and the sorrow in the chamber deepened. Word spread through the palace, and soon the city's night quiet was replaced by hushed lamentations. Courtiers, servants, and warriors alike bowed their heads as if a sudden tempest had passed through their midst.

A small retinue carefully lifted Gilgamesh's body, carrying it to the throne room, a place he had graced with both might and mercy for so many years. There, they laid him on a raised dais, adorning him with the cloak he once wore in triumph, placing tokens of his battles and achievements around him. The hush of the city turned into a long, collective exhale, as men, women, and even children gathered at the palace gates, tears reflecting torchlight on their cheeks.

At dawn's first light, Gilgamesh's mother, Ninsun, arrived in the hall, her expression grave but regal. She approached her son's still form and gently placed a hand on his brow, whispering words known only to gods and those they loved. Her tears fell onto the stone floor, shimmering like drops of liquid moonlight. She stood straight, turning to face the throng of mourners.

"Behold your king," she said in a voice that trembled with sorrow. "He was born of gods and men, and he walked beyond mortal boundaries. Yet even he must rest now, in the quiet of time. This day, we do not simply mourn a king, we honor a mortal who dared to wrestle with fate itself."

The people bowed, their sobs muffled, hearts laden with grief. Slowly, a procession formed with warriors in polished armor, guildsmen with their finest crafts, and families bearing flowers and simple offerings. They filed past Gilgamesh's body, paying final respects. Some pressed tokens of gratitude into his folded hands, others whispered prayers for his journey into the realm of the dead.

Arumak stood at the head of the line, tears unchecked, recalling how Gilgamesh's courage had ended the siege that once threatened Uruk. Another man, an elder craftsman, remembered the times Gilgamesh commissioned new towers and canals, bringing prosperity to the city. A young mother cradling a child whispered thanks that Gilgamesh had protected their future.

Thus the city gathered, weaving a tapestry of love and grief around the memory of its king. Hours stretched into a solemn day of mourning, and by dusk, the palace courtyard was laden with offerings, from grain, woven cloth, engraved tablets, and more. Uruk's highest priests chanted blessings, calling upon the gods to welcome Gilgamesh into the afterlife, that he might find peace in the embrace of ancestors and the memory of Enkidu.

Ninsun, her tears spent, lifted her face to the sky. She alone sensed the last faint echo of her son's spirit, perhaps touching the threshold of eternity. A gentle breeze rustled through the courtyard, stirring the torches so their flames danced in warm halos. In that moment, a hush encompassed all gathered, as though a divine presence acknowledged Gilgamesh's crossing.

By the second dawn, preparations began for Gilgamesh's burial. A grand tomb was fashioned, as befitted a king whose might and compassion had shaped Uruk's destiny. It stood near the banks of the Euphrates, where water was a symbol of life, would forever flow. Within, they placed his armor, his sword, and a carved image of Enkidu kneeling before a lion, a silent testament to their bond. The fragrance of incense filled the air, mingling with the salt of tears.

They laid Gilgamesh to rest with great honor. Uruk's people surrounded the tomb, chanting prayers for his spirit. A hush of finality settled over them as the last stone was placed. In that moment, the city felt a pang of loss so acute it left them breathless, yet beneath it was a current of gratitude and love.

Back within the palace, Ninsun retreated to her temple, the weight of her son's mortality pressing on her heart. She thought of Shamash's words, that even gods would one day face an ending. And she wept, not just for Gilgamesh, but for all living things bound to time's wheel.

In the days that followed, Uruk continued to live, its streets again thrumming with commerce and daily tasks. Yet the city carried a new solemnity, a hush at the edges of its heartbeat that spoke of Gilgamesh's absence. Tales of his deeds were told around cooking fires each night. New epics were composed, new ballads sung, so that in memory, Gilgamesh might remain a guiding force.

Thus the mortal king, born of gods and men, found an immortality no flower could grant, for it was in the hearts that revered his courage and mercy, in the city whose walls he had raised high, in the legacy of love he had chosen over cruelty.

And somewhere, in a realm beyond mortal sight, perhaps Gilgamesh felt the gentle hands of Enkidu clasping his own, guiding him through a house of dust into the light of a new dawn. There, free from the burdens of kingship and sorrow, the two friends embraced, their voices echoing across the silence of ages. And in that cosmic hush, the warrior king at last found the peace he had once sought in vain.